Lakeside Romance

Lisa Jordan

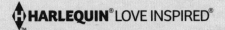

Recycling programs for this product may not exist in your area.

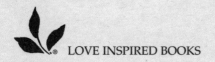

LOVE INSPIRED BOOKS

ISBN-13: 978-0-373-71974-7

Lakeside Romance

Copyright © 2016 by Lisa Jordan

www.Harlequin.com

Printed in U.S.A.

"Wake up, sleepyhead. We're home."

Sarah's eyelids fluttered open. She palmed his cheek. "You're cute."

He grinned. Yep, definitely the painkillers. He guided her out of the car and up the stairs. Once she was settled on the couch, he covered her with the knitted afghan. "Will you be alone today?"

"Just in the evening, but I can hang out at my brother's. The girls think I'm kind of fun."

Not just the girls.

Instead of dwelling on that sudden thought and before common sense kicked in, he spoke. "How about if we hung out at my place? I'll cook dinner, and then we can watch *My Fair Lady.*"

"Will there be popcorn?"

"As long as you're not making it."

She stuck her tongue out at him. "One little smoke alarm…"

She closed her eyes, a smile curving her mouth. Seconds later, her breathing evened out.

Alec closed the door behind him and headed down the steps. The dinner and movie were not a date. Just helping out a friend.

How many times would he have to repeat it for his heart to believe it?

Lisa Jordan has been writing for over a decade, taking a hiatus to earn her degree in early childhood education. By day, she operates an in-home family child-care business. By night, she writes contemporary Christian romances. Being a wife to her real-life hero and mother to two young-adult men overflows her cup of blessings. In her spare time, she loves reading, knitting, and hanging out with family and friends. Learn more about her at lisajordanbooks.com.

Books by Lisa Jordan

Love Inspired

Lakeside Reunion
Lakeside Family
Lakeside Sweethearts
Lakeside Redemption
Lakeside Romance

And we know that in all things God works for the good of those who love him, who have been called according to his purpose.
—*Romans 8:28*

To Scott and Mitchell. Walk with God.
I love you forever.

Acknowledgments

Thanks to Mindy Obenhaus,
Susan May Warren, Beth K. Vogt, Melissa Tagg,
Michelle Lim, Joanne Bischof, Lynn Shultz,
Carolyn Vibbert, Amanda, Sara Patry
and the Coffee Girls for your brainstorming,
feedback and encouragement.

Thanks to Jeanette Walter, Kathy Hurst,
Bill Nobles, Lon and Kayla Hurst,
and Mark "James the Butler" Hurst for the
research help. Any mistakes are mine.

Thanks to Pastors C.D. and Jo Moore
for sharing Truth at the perfect times.

Thanks to Rachelle Gardner, Melissa Endlich
and the Love Inspired team
for bringing my books to print.

To Patrick for being my #1 fan.
Always and forever.

Thank You, Lord, for Your continued blessings.

Chapter One

Sarah needed to get rid of the dress.

Her pity party had gone on way too long. She wasn't the first woman to be dumped, and she wasn't about to let Adam's commitment issues color her against marriage. After all, her brother, Caleb, had managed to find love a second time around with Zoe.

There was hope for Sarah, too.

Someday.

Even if the memories hadn't faded, it was the only way to put the past where it belonged, so she could focus on her future—find a new purpose for her life. Whatever that may be. Holding on to the dress served only as a reminder that she wasn't worth committing to.

For now, though, she'd sell the strapless gown studded with Swarovski crystals and seed pearls on eBay or perhaps find a consignment shop. Wasn't there one in town—Christy's Closet or something like that?

Until she could get rid of it, though, it would still be hanging in her closet...taunting her about her single status.

She couldn't allow that. The dress had to go now.

She wadded the satin creation into a ball, stuffed

it into a garbage bag and tossed it on top of a pile of empty boxes that needed to be recycled first thing in the morning.

Across the room, a breeze carrying the scent of pending rain rippled through the curtains, ushering in the whispers of the night through the window.

With renewed energy, Sarah tore open the flaps of one of the boxes stacked under her window. She pulled out an armful of romance novels, carried them into the living room and stacked them on the shelves of the empty bookcase standing next to her favorite chair. She returned to the bedroom for another load.

Finishing her unpacking now would give her time this weekend to get settled before beginning her new job on Monday—teaching life skills to teenagers in a summer outreach program through her church. She hadn't expected to be adding that to her résumé, but then she'd never anticipated having her life turned upside down, either.

Cool air whisked over her bare arms. Leafy branches scratched at the window. Sarah gathered the books to her chest and pressed her forehead against the pane. The glass chilled her head, but did little to stop the familiar tension headache forming at her temples.

She'd done enough for tonight. It was time to wind down with a cup of tea.

Her stomach rumbled. And apparently a snack.

She pushed away from the window, set the books on the floor, reached for a pink sweatshirt and tugged it over her head, covering her white tank top and blue polka-dot pajama pants.

Feeling her way along the unfamiliar wall of the small second-floor apartment of the old Victorian house she'd moved into this morning, Sarah fumbled for the kitchen light switch. As she flicked on the light, she caught her big toe on the corner of the cabinet. Pain lanced her foot. She bit down on her lower lip to keep from crying out. Releasing a halfhearted string of whimpers, she hobbled over to the counter to turn on her Keurig.

Spying the apartment-warming basket her family had given her after dinner, she waded through ribbons and cellophane to find a package of popcorn. Comfort food—that's what she needed.

While the popcorn popped in the microwave, she searched the white cabinets for the mugs her new sister-in-law, Zoe, had washed and put away. Grabbing her favorite Bartlett University ceramic mug, she dropped a decaf vanilla chai tea bag into the machine, slid her cup under the brewing station and pushed the button. The buttery scent of popcorn wafted her way, causing her stomach to growl even louder.

Once the water finished streaming into the mug, Sarah cupped it, inhaled the rich aroma and pressed her back against the gray L-shaped countertop to survey the newly updated kitchen.

With its white walls and the arched window over the sink, which looked out into the trimmed backyard with its large weeping willow bowing over the stream that sliced through the property, she had fallen in love with this room when she viewed the apartment. Too bad she wore the World's Greatest Cook apron ironically. Otherwise, cooking on the shiny surface of the stainless-steel stove would bring her great pleasure. So would actually having someone to cook for.

Her mother kept telling her she wasn't going to find a husband if she didn't learn to cook. But she didn't even want to think of that right now. She didn't need a guy in her life.

She'd moved to Shelby Lake, the lakefront community in northwestern Pennsylvania, nine months ago—two days after Adam decided to end their engagement six weeks before their wedding. She'd helped her brother with his two young daughters and had pieced together her broken heart with tears and whispered prayers.

Now that Caleb and Zoe had returned from their honeymoon, they needed privacy to blend their families together. And Sarah needed the freedom to explore her future. She'd also concentrate her efforts on making the summer outreach program a success in order for the church board to continue the program on a permanent basis.

A sense of anticipation tickled her sternum.

She took another sip of her tea, then set it on the counter.

Shouldn't that popcorn be almost done?

Sarah glanced at the microwave. Smoke blackened the door. She wrenched it open. Gray billows escaped and spiraled toward the ceiling. She coughed at the acrid smell burning her nostrils and throat.

Burrowing her nose into the collar of her sweatshirt, she grabbed a dish towel and waved the smoke away so she could pull out the charred bag. Heat burned her fingers as she tossed the smoking mess into the sink and turned on the water.

Sarah glanced at the timer on the microwave. Instead of three minutes, she had added an extra zero.

Way to go.

A shrill sound pierced the air.

She threw open the window over the sink, then darted across the room to wave the dish towel in front of the smoke alarm to stop the offending sound before it woke up the neighborhood.

Her arm ached as she stretched on tiptoes and flapped the towel like a hyperactive bird. Once the noise stopped, she sagged against the wall and blew out puffed cheeks.

Heavy footsteps thundering up the stairs and a pounding on her front door jerked her to her feet. A male voice yelled through the steel door. "Open up!"

Heart hammering, she dropped the towel in the sink and raced to the door, then threw it open.

A man stood at the top of the landing dressed in a wrinkled T-shirt, jeans and bare feet. His dark brown hair looked as if he tamed it with a garden rake. Shadows darkened his jaw. With one arm braced against her door frame, he stared at her with eyes the color of faded denim. His nostrils flared as his chest heaved and lips thinned.

She was in so much trouble.

Silently begging her racing heart to settle down, Sarah cleared her throat. "May I help you?" One shaky hand on the doorknob, she rested the other against the frame, shielding the opening with her body.

"Do you always answer the door without checking to see who it is?"

"No. Not usually. I just…well, it's been kind of a crazy night. I wasn't thinking—"

He cut her off by stepping forward and trying to shoulder past her into the apartment.

"Excuse me. What are you doing? You can't come in here." With her heartbeat pounding in her ears, she closed the door partially to block his entrance.

As if she could even take him if he tried to push his way in.

"Where's the fire?" As if realizing what he was doing, the man stepped back, but he reached for her wrist. "The fire department's already on its way. You need to get out where it's safe."

She pulled her hand out of his grasp. Heat crawled up her neck.

Could this night get any worse?

Sirens screamed down the street, becoming louder as they stopped in front of the house. Lights flashed in the darkness at the bottom of her steps.

"There's no fire. I overcooked my popcorn." Sarah jerked a thumb over her shoulder and nodded toward the kitchen.

"Popcorn?" He rubbed a hand over his face, then shook head. "My alarm went off for popcorn? You can't be serious."

His alarm?

Wait a minute. Didn't Mary Seaver, who showed her the place in her grandson's absence, mention interconnecting smoke alarms between the downstairs and upstairs apartments? So that would make this man her downstairs neighbor…and landlord.

Perfect. Absolutely perfect.

After dealing with flight delays, crossing a couple of time zones and spending a week away from work at a real-estate conference, all Alec wanted was a decent night's sleep. But, apparently, that wasn't going to happen tonight.

With hands jammed in his front pockets and bare feet, Alec stood on the sidewalk next to his new neighbor as the fire crew double-checked the upstairs apartment. He tried to tell them it was nothing more than burned popcorn, but since the security company had no-tified them, they needed to do their own investigation.

And he knew that.

But that did little to settle the memories the alarm had awakened in his mind. He forced even breaths into his lungs and exhaled slowly to calm his hammering heart. He could attribute his sweat-slicked skin to the thick-as-fog humidity.

A sweeping glance down the street showed nosy neighbors standing in their yards, gawking at the activity going on in front of his house.

Exactly what he hated—people in his business.

His bones sagged as his eyes burned with fatigue. The pounding in his skull didn't help, either.

Why had Gran rented the upstairs apartment to a scatterbrain?

She'd called him to say a sweet, responsible girl from her church was looking for an apartment for the summer. Despite his hesitation at renting to someone without meeting her first and for only a short time, he'd given in, trusting Gran's judgment. Look where that'd gotten him. With a signed lease and three months' rent paid in advance, he was stuck with the popcorn burner.

His new neighbor—what was her name again?—glanced at him and stuck out her hand. "I'm really sorry for causing so much trouble. I'm Sarah, by the way. Sarah Sullivan. I promise not to be a problem in the future."

Her smile revealed even, white teeth and empha-sized her high cheekbones. The streetlights haloed her short dark hair that stood out at all angles. The top of her head didn't even come to his shoulder. She didn't look old enough to be out of high school, let alone living on her own. Something about her seemed familiar, but in his brain-fogged state, he couldn't place where he'd seen her.

He shook her hand quickly, then released it. "Alec. And that's good to know. I like sleeping at night. You related to Caleb Sullivan?"

"Yes, he's my brother."

That was how he knew her. "He's a good man."

"The best." She looked at him and cocked her head. "Didn't you play at his wedding a couple of weeks ago?"

"I did."

The image of her walking down the aisle in the pale blue halter dress clicked into place.

Billy Lynn, Shelby Lake's battalion chief on duty and Alec's brother-in-law, strode over to them and clapped Alec on the shoulder. "All's clear. I'll phone it in to the security company. You're both free to go back inside."

"Thanks, man." The tinge of smoke that lingered in the material of Billy's turnout gear snaked through Alec, unearthing memories best left buried.

Sarah shot them a quick, apologetic smile. "Again, so sorry. Have a good night." She jogged barefoot across the grass and disappeared into the house.

Billy chuckled and shook his head. "You're going to have your hands full with that one."

"I don't have the time, or the inclination, to deal with anyone."

Billy's lips thinned as he scrubbed a hand over his buzzed head. "You know, Alec, Christy's been gone four years today."

Alec held up a hand. "Stop, okay? I know exactly how long she's been gone."

He didn't need a calendar to know what day it was.

"My sister wouldn't want to see you like this." Billy

crossed his arms over his chest, emphasizing his wrestler's build.

"Yeah, well, she's not here anymore." And he had no one to blame but himself.

"No. No, she isn't." Billy heaved a sigh and moved his helmet to his other arm. "Listen, since I'm already poking the bear...we have an opening in the department, if you'd like to come back."

Alec shook his head and scoffed. "You're in rare form tonight, aren't you?"

Billy shrugged. "What can I say? Haven't seen you in a while, so I figured why not get it all in while I can?"

Alec waved a hand over the yard. "Dude, you know where I live."

"Yeah, I know, buddy."

"I appreciate the offer, but that part of my life is in the past, where it needs to stay." The fire department didn't need a crew member who still battled nightmares or freaked out over smoke alarms.

"Don't even go there, man." Billy's voice snapped like a whip. "You threw away your career because of one house."

Alec's heart smashed against his ribs. "Go there? Dude, I never left. And it wasn't just any house, Billy. You know that. It was *my* house. The one I shared with my wife. The one where we were going to raise our family." His chest tightened as he chugged in ragged breaths. He jammed his fingers through his hair, then locked his hands behind his head.

Billy's shoulders sagged. "I'm sorry, man. I didn't mean to get you riled up. I just hate seeing you merely existing."

"I don't think I've had a decent night's sleep in four years." He mumbled the words mostly to himself. He didn't need to close his eyes to feel flames from the past searing his skin or smell the choking grasp of the thick smoke. Or hear his wife's frantic screams, begging him to save her... He ground the heels of his hands into his eye sockets. "I have a responsibility to my grandparents now."

"It wasn't your fault, Alec." Billy gripped his shoulder.

"Tell that to your mom." Jane Lynn's grief-stricken screams echoed inside the dark chambers of his mind.

You should have saved her! My daughter is dead because of you!

Squeezing his eyes shut, he forced the accusation back behind the locked door of his memory. He glanced longingly toward his front door. "I appreciate your concern. I do, but I'm running on empty. I need to catch some *z*'s."

Billy gave him a long look. "I'm serious, man. Would you want Christy to live like this if she had lost you?"

Of course not, but how could he explain the deep hole in his heart that couldn't be filled by anyone else?

"I know it's been tough. I miss my baby sister every day," Billy continued. "You know, I used to watch you two together and think you were the perfect couple. You'd cook these fantastic meals together, and anytime Etta James came on the radio, you'd pull Christy away from the sink and dance with her. That's what you need—to find another dance partner...someone who makes you laugh and brings back the joy in your life."

Billy stated the impossible. No one could fill his arms...or his heart...the way Christy had. She had been a perfect fit.

He shot a mischievous look at Alec. "If you don't start living—I mean really living instead of going through the motions—then I'm going to pass out your number to every single chick I know…and I know plenty."

Alec's eyes narrowed. "You wouldn't dare."

"Try me."

Alec dropped his chin to his chest a moment, then glared at Billy. "Fine, you win."

The teasing tone dropped out of Billy's voice. "It's not about winning, Alec."

"Yeah." Alec rubbed his thumb and forefinger over eyelids made of burlap. "I really need to hit the hay."

Billy clapped him on the shoulder. "Yeah, okay. We'll talk soon."

"Later." Alec strode across the lawn, his feet and the frayed hems of his jeans dampened by the night dew. He entered his apartment, locking the door behind him.

Instead of heading for his bed, he dropped into the oversize leather chair in the corner of the living room. Swinging a foot onto the matching ottoman, he rested his head against the cushioned back.

The minute the fire alarm had screamed through the stillness of the night, his adrenaline had yanked him out of his sleep. He had thrown on clothes and rushed upstairs. All he could think about was saving the new tenant. He couldn't handle another death on his conscience.

Sitting up, he opened the drawer in the side table and reached for a handful of photos, smudged with fingerprints and creased from being handled. He leafed through them quickly, not really needing the visual reminder of Christy's smile or the way her blue eyes sparkled when she laughed. But, for a moment, he needed to flip through them to remind himself why he couldn't respond differently to Billy's offer.

He paused on the one photo that nearly mangled his

gut each time he looked at it—a candid shot of him and Christy slow dancing in his grandparents' kitchen. They had celebrated their first Christmas together as a married couple with his family. While doing dishes, their wedding song had come on the radio. He asked Christy to dance with him. She'd fit perfectly into his arms. He hadn't minded the way she teased him playfully about his missteps. His sister, Chloe, had taken the picture as he dropped a kiss on the tip of his wife's nose.

The memory only served to hurt him more deeply. Because, as he continued to gaze at the image, a thought invaded his mind. He hadn't just lost his wife and everything they owned in the fire—he'd also lost his unborn son.

Alec dropped the pictures back in the drawer and slammed it shut. He pushed himself out of the chair and wandered down the darkened hall to his bedroom.

More than anything, he wanted to bring back the family he'd lost and have the life he was meant to live. But that was impossible.

If he could turn back the clock, he'd make different choices—choices that would've protected Christy and his baby. As long as the trauma from his past continued to plague him, having a life with anyone else was impossible.

But he couldn't drown out Billy's words. His brother-in-law still remained single, despite his share of dates, so he didn't understand what it was like to love and lose one's partner.

What Alec wouldn't give to laugh again and to have the same kind of happiness he'd shared with Christy.

But dancing ever again?

That was out of the question. No one could fill his arms the way she had.

Chapter Two

This wasn't how Sarah expected to start this new initiative. At least they had a buffer of time until the teenagers started next week. Sarah and Melissa had planned to use this week to finalize any last-minute details, buy supplies and set up the community center for group cooking. But now it looked like she may be on her own.

She parked her dented yellow VW Beetle in the parking garage, grabbed the basket of white daisies and hurried across the lot. The doors to Shelby Lake Memorial swooshed open. The tang of antiseptic spiraled her back to last summer when Dad had spent time in Pittsburgh after suffering a heart attack.

Finding the elevator, she took it to the second floor. She stopped at room 218 and tapped softly. Hearing a faint "come in," she entered and then partially closed the door to drown out the dinging call bells and talking in the hall.

Sunshine spilled through the narrow window, streaking across the pale green walls and glossy tiled floors.

Melissa Kendall, the pastor's wife and her summer outreach program partner, lay in the bed. She was dressed in a hospital gown with an IV pumping fluid into her arm, and her dark hair fanned across the pillow, emphasizing the chalky whiteness of her skin.

Nate, Melissa's husband and Sarah's pastor, slumped in an uncomfortable position in a chair next to the bed, eyes closed, his hand resting on his wife's.

Eyes drowsy, Melissa managed a weak smile. "Hey."

"When you suggested we get together this morning to talk about the program, you failed to mention the new meeting spot." Sarah smiled to show she was joking.

"Yeah, well, you know me—Queen of the Last-Minute Changes. Pretty flowers."

"I figured they'd cheer you up." Sarah set the flowers on the windowsill and moved over to the bed. She squeezed Melissa's fingers. "When you didn't show up at the community center or answer your phone, I called Nate's secretary, Cindy, to see if you were at the church. She told me where to find you."

Pulling her hand out of her husband's grasp, Melissa tried to sit up but winced and dropped back on the pillow. Lines tightened around her mouth. "I didn't feel so hot in church yesterday, and then after lunch, I started having some nausea and stomach pains. Last night I doubled over, so Nate called the ambulance. Once we arrived, I was rushed into surgery for an emergency appendectomy."

"I'm so sorry. How are you feeling now?"

"Tired, and a little sore. I woke up in pain a little while ago, and the nurse gave me something, but it hasn't kicked in yet." Melissa's eyelids fluttered as if she were fighting sleep to talk.

"Who's staying with Little Nate?"

"He's with Mom and Dad."

Sarah smoothed Melissa's hair away from her forehead. "Is there anything I can do?"

Tears welled up in Melissa's eyes and seeped over the curve of her face.

"Hey, it will be okay." Sarah opened the small box of hospital tissues and handed one to Melissa.

Melissa wiped her eyes and shook her head. "All those months and months of planning, and now our summer program is coming to a halt."

Sarah's heart picked up speed. "What do you mean 'coming to a halt'? Did the program lose funding?"

"Nothing like that." Melissa shook her head, then offered a wobbly smile. "I'm pregnant, Sarah."

"Oh, that's great! Right?"

"Yes, of course." She dropped her gaze to her hands and tore the tissue into small pieces. "But with the emergency surgery, my doctor wants me on bed rest for the next few weeks to ensure I don't lose this baby."

Nate stirred and looked around the room a little confused. Then he stretched, stifled a yawn and nodded to Sarah. "Hey, Sarah."

"Hi. I hear congratulations are in order."

He shot a worried glance at Melissa but couldn't hide the smile creeping across his face. "Yeah, thanks."

He leaned over the bed and brushed a kiss across his wife's temple. "How are you feeling, babe?"

"Sore. Tired."

"Close your eyes and rest." Nate stood and stretched again. "I need to find some coffee. Sarah, care to join me?"

Sarah cast a quick look at her friend only to find her struggling to stay awake. "Sure." She leaned over the bed and gave Melissa a gentle hug. "Don't worry. Just focus on getting better."

Nate grazed his fingers across Melissa's cheek.

"We're going down to the cafeteria. We'll be back shortly. Love you."

"Love you, too." Her voice slurred as she tried but failed to keep her eyes open.

Sarah headed for the door and waited in the hall for Nate. He joined her, dragging his hands through his hair. Dark circles smudged his eyes. Morning stubble darkened his jaw. His wrinkled polo shirt and shorts showed he hadn't left his wife's side.

"Long night, huh?"

"Yeah, you could say that. The pain meds have kicked in, so Mel's going to be out for a while. Let's hit the cafeteria for some coffee and food."

"As long as you don't mind being away from her."

"I do, but I need to check on Little Nate and call Cindy to cancel my appointments for the rest of the day."

"Nate, is there anything I can do?"

He stabbed the ground floor button on the elevator panel, then shoved his hands in the pockets of his cargo shorts before bracing a shoulder against the wall. "Yes, but I need coffee so I can speak coherently."

As the elevator made the trip toward the main level, Sarah wondered if she should be concerned about Melissa's anxiety over the demise of the program. Or was she stressing because she couldn't help? Hopefully Nate could shed some light on the situation. If they were truly thinking about canceling, maybe she could get him to reconsider. Not just for the community's sake and for all the kids signed up, but for her sake, as well. She needed the income to hold her over for the summer. Plus, the next three months would help her figure out what she wanted to do with her life.

The scents of breakfast beckoned them toward the

hot-foods station, where Nate heaped a plate with eggs and several slices of bacon. Sarah filled two foam cups with coffee. Nate paid for the food, and then they found an empty table toward the back of the hospital cafeteria.

After praying over his food, he shoveled a forkful of eggs into his mouth. A few more bites and a couple slurps of coffee later, he wiped his mouth and sat back in his chair. "Now I feel a little more human."

"You've had a rough night." She stirred creamer into her coffee.

He pushed the rest of the eggs around the paper plate. "Yeah, she had me pretty scared for a while."

Sarah reached for his hand and gave it a quick squeeze. "She'll be fine, Nate."

"I know." Pushing his tray aside, he leaned forward and rested his arms on the table. "So you're getting settled in your new place?"

"Yes, it's been an…interesting weekend. Met my landlord." No need to tell Nate about the popcorn…she wanted to convince him to keep the program.

"Alec Seaver's a good man. He's been through a lot. Don't let his gruff get to you."

Remembering her landlord's stony glare, she stored that bit of info away. She wanted to ask more but knew Nate wouldn't spill what wasn't his to share. One more thing she respected about her pastor.

"Listen, Sarah, I need to talk to you about the summer outreach program."

Her hands tightened around her cup. "Sure, what's up?"

"This is such a great opportunity for our church to reach beyond its doors and connect with the kids who don't attend regularly or at all. You and Mel have done a ton of planning. It's scheduled to begin next week with Mel teaching the bulk of the cooking portion of the program, right?"

Sarah picked up the plastic stirrer and twisted it into a knot. "Yes, very few people have Melissa's cooking talents."

"I wasn't a fool to marry a woman with mad culinary skills." A smile tugged at his mouth as he patted his trim stomach.

Sarah laughed. "Very smart move on your part, my friend."

Nate's smile disappeared. "I talked with the doctor after Melissa's surgery. This pregnancy surprised all of us. We're thrilled, but we're also concerned because she's already had two miscarriages since Little Nate was born. The doctor wants to keep her activities limited for the next couple of months to ensure she'll be out of danger. Mel's parents and her brother and sister-in-law have already offered to do what's necessary to help us."

"It's always great to have a supportive family." Sarah's heart panged a little. Other than Caleb and Zoe, she didn't really know what that entailed. "What can I do to help?"

"I need to know if you can handle the program by yourself. We still have church members signed up each week as volunteers to lend a hand, so you won't be all by yourself. Plus, I'll be in every morning to do the daily devotional like we talked about. Melissa's stressing out about losing this outreach opportunity. If she knows you're willing to continue the program without her, then she'll relax."

"Yes, Nate, of course. Whatever you need me to do, I'll do it."

"Great. Because backing out is not really an option." Nate drained his cup and stood, grabbing the tray. "I appreciate everything you're doing, Sarah. Like I said when I hired you—if this program is a success, the board wants to make it a full-time opportunity. That way we can help these kids way past summer, even if it's only for a couple of hours after school. They need to know they matter."

Sarah followed Nate out of the cafeteria, chewing on his final words. She'd figure out a way to get through the cooking portion of the program, even if it meant reading dozens of cookbooks, viewing YouTube videos or binge-watching the Food Network. It couldn't be that hard. After all, a bunch of teenagers wouldn't be expecting Rachael Ray, right?

She couldn't let her church family down...or the kids involved in the program.

If only life's problems could be solved with a pot of soup.

Alec lifted the lid and stirred the heavy cream into the zuppa Toscana bubbling on the stove. He tossed in two large handfuls of chopped kale, gave it another stir and then topped the pot with the lid to let everything simmer for about ten more minutes. The aroma of cooked sausage and fried bacon mingled with the chopped onion and pressed garlic.

Ella Fitzgerald crooned from his docked iPhone on the counter. He hummed along as she sang about someone watching over her.

The timer on his bread maker beeped. After turning the machine off, Alec reached for a pot holder, pulled the bread pan out and turned over the steaming loaf of Italian herb bread onto the metal cooling rack.

The doorbell pealed, sending his shoulders to his ears. He made another mental note to install a different, less intrusive sounding one.

Swallowing a sigh, he dropped the pot holder on the counter and wiped his hands on a dish towel before heading to the door.

He'd left the front door open, allowing the afternoon breeze to sweep in through the screen door. He saw a woman's silhouette on the porch. Too tall to be his sister. Besides, Chloe would knock once and come in without waiting for an invitation. Or come in through the back door.

The woman turned, and his steps slowed. His new tenant stood on his welcome mat, her arms wrapped around a stack of books, and a wide smile emphasized those incredible cheekbones.

"Can I help you?"

She shifted the books and pulled a hand free to give him a little wave. "Hi, Alec…right?"

He nodded, but didn't say anything more.

"Yeah, well, I checked my mail and found a letter addressed to you in my box." She pulled an envelope off the stack of books and thrust it at him.

He took it, caught the return address—Shelby Lake County Juvenile Detention Center—and his gut tightened. He shoved it in his back pocket, planning to add it to the rest later. "Thanks for dropping it off."

"You're welcome." She turned away from the door and started across the porch. Before he could close the door, she turned back to him. "You're probably going to think I'm a nut or something, but I could smell something amazing coming from your place, so I wondered who did your cooking." Her words tumbled over her lips so quickly and without a breath in between that Alec was thankful she didn't just pass out from the effort.

"My cooking?"

She shrugged. "Yeah, I mean, something smells so great."

Was she wrangling for an invitation?

"I do my own cooking."

"You made…" She paused, lifted her nose and inhaled deeply a moment before letting out the pent up breath slowly. A smile spread easily across her face as if it was something she did often. "It smells fantastic. What is it, by the way?"

"Zuppa Toscana and Italian herb bread."

"Sounds like something you'd get in a restaurant. My friend Melissa is an amazing cook, too." Sarah shifted the load in her arms again. Alec caught a glimpse of one of the titles and recognized it as a cookbook he had sitting on the shelf next to his fridge. "Would you like a job?"

He scowled "A job? I have a job."

"Right." She waved a hand as if dismissing her offer. "I'm sure you do. This isn't even a regular job. Especially since you wouldn't get paid."

"That sounds really appealing." He folded his arms over his chest and pressed a shoulder against the doorjamb.

She laughed, a sound that stirred a dormant feeling inside him. "Actually it's a temporary volunteer position. I'm overseeing a new summer outreach program through the youth ministry at my church. We're helping teenagers learn basic life skills such as cooking, cleaning, budgeting, etcetera. My program partner, who is this amazing chef, had emergency surgery last night, so now she won't be able to do the cooking portion of the program. And, well, as you saw last night with the popcorn fiasco, I'm not exactly Martha Stewart."

Did this woman ever breathe between sentences? Another time, he might've found her rambling endearing...

He straightened and reached for the stack of books. He turned them over to read the titles on the spines, then curled them into the crook of his arm. "Did Billy put you up to this?"

"Who?" She shot him a questioning look.

"Never mind. So let me see if I'm understanding you correctly... You're looking for someone to help you teach teenagers to cook?"

She rubbed her hands over the red creases the stack of books had left on her arms. "Yes, actually. Are you interested?"

Placing his free hand in the front pocket of his jeans, he laughed and shook his head. "No. Not in a million years, sister."

"But—" Her brows knitted together.

"I'm sorry." He handed the cookbooks back to her. "If you'll excuse me, I have to take some food to my uncle."

Even though Gran would lecture him on his rudeness, he closed the door and walked back to the kitchen, not waiting to see if his babbling neighbor continued to stand on his front porch.

The last thing in the world he wanted was to hang out with a bunch of teenagers. No, thank you. He wasn't going down that road again.

He flicked the heat off under the sputtering soup, stirred it a final time and then ladled some into several glass bowls. After packing the single servings into a shallow box along with the bread, Alec carried the food out the back kitchen door and followed the sidewalk trailing behind his house to the garage.

He dropped the food off to Uncle Emmett at the

Lakeside Suites and spent forty minutes listening to Emmett grumble about getting kicked out of his home. In an effort to placate him, Alec promised to stop by the house to get a particular book. Having moved into the assisted-living apartment last weekend, Uncle Emmett still insisted he needed certain things from his home, despite the family's insistence that he downsize.

Alec unlocked the dead bolt and pushed open the front door of the yellow house with white trim and a wraparound porch. The scent of neglect and abandonment permeated the air. Or maybe that was Alec's guilt eating at him. Maybe he should've tried harder to help Emmett stay in his home. But the decision was out of his hands and it wouldn't have solved the problem—Emmett's doctor said his uncle's health required assisted living.

Despite the midafternoon sunshine, darkness shrouded the room. He pushed back the outdated drapes and hefted open the window, hearing the pulley weights thunk, and then stepped back to allow waves of fresh air to filter out the staleness. Sunlight straddled the stacks of magazines and towers of books while dust motes scattered across the heavy maple furniture that had been as much a part of this house as the occupants.

Uncle Emmett and Aunt Elsie had purchased this house over fifty years ago, but after Aunt Elsie's death, Emmett couldn't bring himself to make any changes, including canceling her subscriptions to her favorite painting magazines.

With their only child having been born with Down syndrome, Uncle Emmett needed someone to oversee his assets. In case anything happened to him, Emmett had signed the house over to Alec years ago. He'd done so with the promise that Alec would sell it and ensure the money went into Gideon's special-needs trust so he could continue living at Jacob House, a local residential home for adult men who required special care.

Alec searched the shelves, found the book his uncle had requested, closed the windows and then let himself out of the house, locking the door behind him.

Half an hour later, he parked his car in his garage. With the engine still idling, he pressed his head against the headrest and sighed. A jazzy tune crooned from the satellite radio station, but the upbeat tempo did little to raise Alec's mood.

An unsettling feeling knotted his stomach. After returning the requested books, he'd had another conversation—more like an argument—with Uncle Emmett about Alec's desire to get the Dutch Colonial home listed quickly. Getting it on the market by the end of summer needed to be his highest priority, but he couldn't even think about listing it until the place was cleaned out and repaired. The higher the selling price, the more money for Gideon.

He just didn't see how he could find the time to get it done. He could talk with Gran and Chloe to see if they'd be able to pitch in, but Gran wouldn't be able to do the heavy lifting and constant bending at her age. Plus, between teaching piano lessons, running church activities and spending time with her Tea Grannies—a group of older women at her church who made it their mission to play matchmaker to the singles in the community—he couldn't ask her to help out. His sister had her hands full with her early-learning child care center, especially with her annual state inspection coming up. Maybe he'd have to consider hiring someone, but bringing in an outsider to rummage through his family's things didn't really sit well with him.

He'd find someone… He had no choice.

Climbing out of his car, he closed the door, silencing the trumpet sounds from the radio. He glanced at the yellow Beetle parked in the other stall.

Wait a minute…

What if he *did* agree to teach his neighbor to cook? Would she be willing to help him out in return? But asking her was crazy. He knew nothing about her.

But Gran and Chloe knew her. After learning about the fire-alarm episode, both reassured him Sarah wouldn't be any trouble. They'd spent the next twenty minutes singing her praises.

He did know her brother, and Caleb was an upstanding guy, not to mention a Shelby Lake police officer.

Maybe asking wouldn't be so bad. She could always say no.

He took the stairs to Sarah's apartment two at a time and rapped his knuckles against the door.

Music blared. A crash sounded, then a muffled cry before the door was wrenched open.

His neighbor greeted him with something brown splattered across the front of her shirt.

"Bad time?"

She popped a hand on her hip and cocked her head. "You know, I don't think there's ever a good time when you put me in the kitchen. Come in." Pulling the door open, she moved aside to let him in.

He stepped inside and slid out of the way so she could close the door. "I don't want to keep you from…whatever it is you're doing—"

She pushed hair off her face with the back of her wrist and glanced toward the kitchen. "Creating a disaster, apparently."

"I stopped by with a proposal for you."

She lowered her head, batted her eyes and fanned herself with her hand. "Why, Mr. Seaver, it's a bit sudden, don't you think? We've only known each other a few days."

He rolled his eyes and shook his head. What a scatterbrain. Maybe this wasn't a good idea after all, but he was running out of options. He braced his hand against the door frame. "I need help getting a house ready to list on the market by the end of summer. You need someone to teach you how to cook. What do you say about helping each other out?"

Her eyes widened. "Are you serious?"

"More than you know."

"Why the change of heart?"

"I don't have a lot of options right now." Alec dragged a hand through his hair. "Someone is relying on me. I won't go back on my word."

"That makes two of us." Sarah crossed her arms and tapped her index finger against her chin. Then she flashed a bright smile. "I'll do it. I'll help with your house, and you can help my teenagers learn to cook."

He lifted a hand. "What? No. I said I'd teach you to cook. It's up to you to pass your skills on to them."

She shrugged. "But I'd need you in the kitchen with me so I don't screw things up or set off more smoke alarms. Two hours each afternoon, and I'll give you the same amount of time each evening with your house."

More than anything, he wanted to turn around and head back down the stairs, taking his absurd idea with him, but he couldn't handle having the same argument every time he visited his uncle. "Fine. I'll give you a few basic lessons, and I'll be on hand to help you out."

"Really? Just so there's no misunderstanding— you're sure you want to do this?"

Want to? Of course not. But he needed help. "Yes, I'll be a regular ole Henry Higgins."

"Who?" She frowned.

"Henry Higgins. You know—the professor from *My Fair Lady* who taught Eliza Doolittle how to speak properly."

Sarah wrinkled her nose. "I'm not crazy about old movies."

"Not old. Classic. Apparently you have more to learn than cooking."

"When would you like to start?"

He glanced at the stain spreading across her shirt. "The sooner, the better by the look of things."

Sarah stuck out her hand. "I accept your proposal, Professor Higgins."

Alec shook her hand.

What had he just agreed to?

Chapter Three

If Sarah didn't need Alec's help so badly, she'd turn around and walk out the door. When he'd suggested cooking lessons in exchange for preparing his uncle's house to be placed on the market, he hadn't mentioned she'd be walking into an episode of *Hoarders*. Maybe for good reason.

And now he stood behind her, blocking her escape.

She set her bucket of cleaning supplies on the floor by the door and moved deeper into the abyss, wrinkling her nose. The air settled around her with the odor of mildew and vapor rub. The wooden floor creaked beneath her flip-flops as she stepped carefully onto a bare spot on the worn area carpet. She balanced herself on one foot while she searched for another space to step.

The image of jumping from rock to rock to cross the stream behind her childhood home slid out from a closeted corner in her mind. Finding there was no free floor space to move to, Sarah put her other foot down almost on top of her first, stayed put and turned in a slow circle to take in every angle of the cluttered living room.

Her gaze roamed over the rows of books spilling from the natural oak cases built around the door frame.

Mismatched framed watercolor paintings in various sizes hung on the faded floral-papered wall behind a couch buried under throw pillows and knitted afghans. Towering stacks of magazines and newspapers lined a narrow path that led into another room. Heavy drapes concealed the sunshine that peaked through the gap and begged to light up the room.

She tried to keep her jaw from gaping like a trout, but she doubted she'd succeeded. A shudder shimmied down her spine.

She wasn't trying to judge, but she just couldn't wrap her head around the chaos. Sure, she needed things organized and put in their places. Otherwise, her brain simply couldn't function. And obviously not everyone had to be like her, but still… Seriously, how did people live like this?

She dragged her fingers through her hair, then waved a hand over the room and looked at Alec. "I'm not gonna lie—I expected some light housekeeping. Maybe some basic organization. Or even some staging. But this…"

Even as her voice trailed off, the knots in her stomach cinched tighter. She needed the outreach program to be a success, but if those teens depended on her to help them cook, they were all in trouble. Somehow she'd have to figure out how to tackle this job.

Did Alec hope she'd take one look at his uncle's house and bail? Set her up to fail so he could get out of helping her? If so, why even bother extending the offer? But he seemed so sincere, almost desperate.

He stuffed his hands in his pockets and pushed away from the wall separating the entryway from the living room. "I know. Uncle Emmett was a bit of a pack rat."

"Pack rat?" She laughed and shook her head. "Alec, I'm sorry to say, but this borders on hoarding."

"Oh, come on. It's not that bad."

"Okay, maybe not, but there's no way I can have this house ready quickly, especially with everything else going on at the moment. Has it always been like this?"

"No." Alec moved behind her into the living room. "After my aunt Elsie died and my cousin Gideon moved into Jacob House, Uncle Emmett couldn't bring himself to cancel her magazine subscriptions. And she wasn't here to pick up after him or nag him to get rid of things. Little by little, things piled up. He surrounded himself with memories of her."

"How long were they married?"

"Forty-eight years."

"That's a long time."

"Yeah. Emmett is actually my great-uncle. His wife was my grandmother's oldest sister, but we've always been close."

Yeah, she could see that. "Where's your uncle right now?"

"Visiting his son, Gideon, at Jacob House, but he moved recently to the Lakeside Suites. Those apartments are small, so he had to downsize drastically."

Sarah moved to the couch and sat on the edge. She rested her elbows on her knees and cupped her jaw. "So how do we pack up forty-eight years of memories?"

"Emmett asked the same thing."

"What did you tell him?" She peered up at him.

He shrugged. "I didn't have an answer."

Neither did she.

Standing, she waved a hand over the piles of magazines. "What are you thinking of doing with all of this stuff…all of these memories?"

"Uncle Emmett took a few things with him like his favorite recliner, a few photos, a couple of Aunt Elsie's watercolors, one of her knitted afghans and some of his favorite books. The rest will have to be boxed up and stored for now."

"And then what? Instead of storing everything, what about donating it or maybe have an estate sale? That way you won't have to deal with it later. And quite honestly, some of it needs to go in a Dumpster or be taken to a recycling center."

Alec tossed his hands in the air and walked away, his back to her. "Oh, sure, let's just pile everything on the front yard and let strangers root through his things."

She put her fisted hands on her hips and rolled her eyes. "Puh-lease. That's not what I meant, and you know it. You asked for my help... It was just a suggestion." She moved to the bookcase and removed a couple of volumes. Running her hand over the embossed covers, she turned and held one up to him. "These books are gorgeous. Some are in excellent condition. You might be able to find a collector interested in purchasing them."

"How can we give it all away like the memories mean nothing?" Alec dragged a hand through his hair, then scrubbed a hand over his face. "You know what? This was a mistake. Thanks for taking the time to come by, but I don't think this arrangement is going to work. I'll figure out something else. I'm sorry for wasting your time."

Sarah slipped the books back in place and held her palms up to him. "Now just hold on a minute. I'm not going to walk away just because you're ticked at my suggestions...suggestions you asked for, by the way. I meant no offense. Let's just chill a minute and figure this out."

She wasn't about to let him walk out on her now. She would see this through. Prove to him she could do this.

Alec walked over to the fireplace and picked up a framed decades-old candid shot of his aunt and uncle sitting on the dock at the Shelby Lake beach. "This was their first house—their only house—as a couple. I spent so much time here when I was growing up. To see it stripped piece by piece and sold for quarters at a yard sale… I can see why Uncle Emmett hated to leave."

"This stuff…" Sarah picked her way to the fireplace to stand next to him. She waved a hand around the room. "They're just things. Yes, it's so easy to get emotionally attached, but they're temporary objects. The memories will last forever."

He held his silence for a moment, as if thinking over her words. "You're right," he finally said. "I spent the morning convincing Emmett he needed to let go of the past. Here I am going on like an idiot. I guess we're both sentimental fools." He returned the photo to the mantel.

Sarah touched his arm. "There's nothing wrong with that as long as you don't allow your past to keep you from facing your future."

Alec needed to relax, but how could he when he had to teach this woman basic skills in just a few days? She'd burned popcorn. And now she expected to have enough skills to teach a bunch of kids? At least he'd be around to supervise.

He didn't have time for these lessons, but he wasn't about to go back on his word, especially since Sarah had battled him to help with his uncle's house even after he'd freaked out on her. Man, he was an idiot. Once they finished with the house and the cooking lessons, he'd put some necessary distance between them.

Truth be told, he wasn't used to having a woman in his kitchen. At least, not *this* kitchen. With the brick backsplash, cabinets painted a shade of navy that reminded him of Shelby Lake, copper countertops and the wood laminate flooring, it looked nothing like the bright and airy white kitchen he'd shared with Christy for almost two years.

That was the point.

The only part he'd brought from his past into this new space was his continued love of cooking to music.

But not today. With Sarah in his kitchen, the radio stayed off so he could focus on teaching her.

At first he'd worried he was getting more out of their bargain, but jerking his eyes back to the present showed him a messy mound of onions that stretched across the cutting board and looked nothing like the small pile he'd cut to demonstrate.

"No, Sarah, don't hack the onion. Cut it." Alec didn't mean for his voice to sound so harsh, but patience wasn't always his strong suit.

Sarah's head jerked up. "I am."

"No, you're not. You're beating it with the blade of your knife. Let me show you again." Alec reached for another, plopped it on the cutting board, and then stood next to Sarah. "Slice it through the root. If you cut it off, it'll start to bleed, and that's what causes you to cry. Allow the weight of your knife to work for you. Then place the onion flat on the board. Keep your knife pointed toward the root and slice through it. Solid strokes. Then turn your knife and slice through the middle and top. Hold everything together and slice evenly. You'll end up with nicely diced pieces."

Instead of copying him with the other half of the onion, she turned and looked up at him. Thick lashes fringed her eyes—eyes so close he could see the burst of sunlight in the field of green. Freckles dotted the bridge of her nose. Her lips parted slightly as if she were about to say something. If he lowered his head—

He jerked his thoughts out of dangerous territory. What was he doing? Why was he even thinking that way? How could he do that to Christy? To the life they shared? The blatant betrayal of his late wife's memory speared his gut.

He released the knife and stepped back. "Uh, do it like that, and you'll have even cuts instead of liquefying your onions."

Sarah dropped her gaze to the pile on the cutting board. "Yeah, I'll, um, do it that way."

She turned back to the counter and picked up the knife. Her cuts slowed and were more meticulous.

Alec washed his hands, then gripped the edge of the sink. The rhythmic tapping of the knife competed with the rain pelting the open kitchen window above the sink. A breeze drifted across the sill and ruffled her already tousled hair. His blue apron fell almost to her knees, but it didn't quite cover her white T-shirt and yellow skirt.

A couple of minutes later, the chopped pile grew. "Onions are diced. Now what?" She laid the knife down and then moved to the sink to wash her hands, her arm brushing his.

He stepped away, giving her some room. "Leave them there for a couple of minutes. Now we need to slice the sausage. Do you remember what I said about slicing?"

She raised an eyebrow and dropped a hand on her hip. "I'm not a total idiot, you know. I do know how to slice."

He grabbed another board and set it in front of her. "Fine, then let's get to it. This soup's not going to make itself."

For their first lesson, Sarah had requested that they make the same zuppa Toscana he'd made for Uncle Emmett. After showing her how to read the recipe and explaining which cooking tools to use, they'd made a list of the ingredients, which Sarah had picked up at the store.

Having her in his kitchen might have been a mistake. But if he was going to teach her to cook, he needed the right tools—his tools. Her knives consisted of a paring knife and a couple of serrated steak knives. If only he could get rid of her fragrance of wildflowers, which was wafting through the room, curling through him and flaying open those wounds best left covered.

She pulled the link of Italian sausage out of the package and flopped it onto the cutting board. She picked up the French knife and started to cut.

"Not that knife." Alec pulled a utility knife out of the block and handed it to her, handle first. "Try this one. You'll have more control as you slice through the sausage. Be careful—it's sharp. How did you become an adult without learning to cook?"

She took the knife and started sawing at the sausage. "Growing up we had a housekeeper who prepared our meals. Mrs. Nelson wouldn't allow anyone in *her* kitchen. When I left home, I ate in the dorm cafeteria, ordered takeout or lived on cereal and freezer meals."

He shook his head. "You have so much to learn. Frozen foods are filled with sodium and preservatives. You need to cook nutritious meals." Catching her action, he stifled a groan and schooled his tone. She wouldn't learn if he kept barking at her. "It's not a log, Sarah. You don't need to saw it. That knife is sharp. Pierce the casing with the tip of the knife and slice through it in a single cut. Like this." He took the knife from her and demonstrated. Just as he'd done with the onion. After handing it back to her, he pressed his back against the sink to watch. Once he was sure she wasn't going to lose an appendage, he turned around to wash the other cutting board.

"How did you learn to cook?"

He dried the cutting board, then slid it back into place on the shelf between his stove and refrigerator. "By reading recipe books and watching cooking shows on TV. I did it to help out my mom after my dad was killed, but then I found out I enjoyed it."

"You lost your dad? I'm sorry."

"Thanks. He was a marine killed in friendly fire when I was fifteen."

The knife clattered against the board as Sarah sucked in a sharp breath. "You weren't kidding about the knife being sharp."

"I don't kid about knives." He turned to see her about to bring her bleeding index finger to her mouth. He grabbed her hand. "No, don't. You've been handling raw pork."

Still holding on to her, he pulled her to the sink and flipped on the water. He pumped hand soap onto her palm. "Wash your hands while I grab a Band-Aid."

Sarah lathered her hands and rinsed. "It's a minor cut. I'll wrap a paper towel around it."

"You're working with food. It needs to be clean and covered." Alec folded a paper towel and pressed it against the cut. "Hold this to get the bleeding stopped. I'll be right back."

He strode down the hall to the master bathroom. Rummaging through the medicine cabinet for the box of bandages, he kicked himself for letting his mind wander. He should've known better than to get distracted. If he lost focus, then someone got hurt.

He pulled out the last two and tossed the empty box in the trash. Leaving the bathroom, he turned off the light. As he passed his dresser, Christy smiled at him from her crystal frame.

His breath caught in his chest, and he nearly dropped to his knees. The Band-Aids fluttered from his fingers. He reached down and picked them up, then braced himself against the doorway. Sarah's humming drifted down the hall.

Why had he invited her into his kitchen?

His lonely, vacant life of going through the motions without Christy wore on him, but he'd had his chance at love once. He couldn't risk his heart a second time. The pain of losing her had gutted him. And he couldn't go through that again. He needed to keep his distance from Sarah.

Chapter Four

Keep it simple, Sarah.

How many times had Alec repeated that phrase over the past week?

Simple. Right.

She glanced at the clock hanging over the sink. Where was he anyway? He promised to be here an hour ago. She'd tried to stall as long as she could, but the teens were getting antsy.

The group of twenty teenagers, aged thirteen to eighteen, were assembled in the Shelby Lake community center kitchen and were currently swatting each other with dish towels and singing into spatulas as if they were auditioning for *The Voice*. Daniel Obenhaus and his brother, Toby, stood off to the side, talking to each other while taking in the ruckus created by everyone else.

Sarah pulled in a deep breath and raised her hands in the air. "Hey, everyone, let's settle down and get back to work. Now it's time to practice some of what we learned this morning."

Once she had all eyes watching her, she shot another glance at the clock, murmured a silent prayer and pulled cartons of eggs out of the industrial-sized side-by-side refrigerator. She set them in the middle of the long worktable in the middle of the room, opened a carton and reached for an egg. "This morning we talked about the importance of good nutrition. Eggs are cheap, and they offer protein and nutrients. I'm going to demonstrate how to crack one." She hit it gently on the edge of the bowl and pried the shell apart. The whites and yolks slid into the stainless-steel bowl without taking even a sliver of shell with it. She smiled and resisted breaking out into a happy dance. At home, she'd even attempted cracking them with one hand the way Alec did and managed not to create too much of a mess.

Scanning the group surrounding three sides of the table, she picked up the whisk, and then she beat the yolk into the white. "This is called beating the egg. We're adding air into our egg mixture while getting it as smooth as possible. You can use a whisk like I am, or a fork…either one works."

Fifteen-year-old Amber Jennings, whose dad worked at the Shelby Lake Police Department with Sarah's brother, Caleb, tossed her blond braid over her shoulder and raised her hand. "Miss Sarah, my mom just like cracks the eggs into the skillet and scrambles them with a spatula. Why do we need to like mess around with bowls and whisks and stuff? Makes more dishes to wash."

"Amber, your mom's way is totally fine. And I hear you about having extra dishes to wash. But beating isn't just for eggs. As we progress throughout the summer, we'll create other dishes that use this technique, so if you learn how to do it in the beginning, then we can continue to build upon those skills to make more challenging dishes." Or at least that's what Alec said when he'd reviewed the lessons with her. Hopefully her words carried more confidence than she felt.

"The only time anything gets beaten in my house is when my old man goes on a bender." Brushing his shaggy brown hair out of his eyes, seventeen-year-old Garrett laughed and elbowed the kid next to him. "Know what I'm saying?"

Despite the kid's teasing tone, truth sliced through his words. In her career of working with youth, Sarah had seen too many bruises that came with ready excuses. She'd have to keep a watchful eye on this group. These kids weren't young men and women she'd been associating with on a regular basis through the church's youth ministry. Most of them didn't attend church. But she hoped to forge those lasting relationships by the end of the summer and draw them into her youth group.

Having worked with youth in community outreach programs in her former church, Sarah had approached Pastor Nate and Melissa with her idea after Christmas—instead of inviting kids and hoping they would come to church and get involved in the youth program, she suggested the church go to them and offer life skills they could take back to their families. Melissa jumped at the idea immediately. They'd spent months securing grants, preparing the curriculum, rounding up volunteers and spreading the word.

Sarah exchanged a quick look with Mindy, her volunteer for the week, and waited a moment until she captured Garrett's gaze. She smiled, but the firmness of her voice relayed the promise in her words. "Garrett, the only beatings happening here are the ones with the food."

His eyes dropped to the toes of his beat-up purple Converse shoes, but then his head jerked up and a smile spread across his face. He shoved a hand in the pocket of his baggy shorts and waved at her with the other. "Aw, Miss Sarah, I was just messin' with you."

She reached for another egg and rolled it in her hand. "How about you start messing with this egg and show me some of those smooth skills I know you've got?"

Garrett swaggered to the table, amid his friend's heckling and hooting, trying to act as if he was doing her a favor, but for a second, he looked at her with softened eyes as if to thank her for the reassurance of her words.

She gave him a barely discernible nod and handed him the egg, giving his fingers a slight squeeze in the exchange. She stepped back, giving him a little space, and watched as he broke the egg with one hand and then beat it smooth with practiced strokes.

"Great job, Garrett. This isn't your first time, is it?"

"Nah, my mom…she works in the kitchen at the Lakeside Lodge. I've been cooking since I was a little kid."

"Great. You'll be a huge help this summer." She pointed to the stacks of stainless-steel bowls and a basket of whisks. "Okay, friends, grab your bowls and whisks. Let's practice beating your eggs."

The sounds of eggs being cracked against bowls and the scraping of whisks against stainless steel filled the oversize kitchen. Whites splashed across the table and a couple of yolks landed on the floor.

Sarah pressed her back against the counter and tried not to glance at the clock for the third time in ten minutes. Crossing her arms over her chest to tamp down the building frustration at Alec, she gave the teens space to do as directed. "Once your eggs are beaten, I'll show you how to scramble them."

Some of the teens were siblings like Daniel and Toby, who lived with their grandma and attended her church. Others were only children. And some like Amber, who had working parents and younger brothers and sisters at home, could benefit from the skills being learned over the summer.

And while they were here, with her, they were safe. If they learned nothing else this summer, they'd know they were loved. And worthy. They mattered. That was one aspect of the program she guaranteed.

A throat clearing behind her caused her to jump. She turned to find Alec standing in the doorway, wearing a red polo shirt with *Seaver Realty* embroidered on it. With a tight smile on his face, he shoved his hands in his tan trouser pockets.

Instead of jumping down his throat at his lateness, she smiled and schooled her tone. "Hey, glad you could make it."

"Yeah, sorry I'm late. Something came up at work." His gaze darted around the room, his jaw clenching. "How's it going?"

She waved a hand over the crowd. "We haven't set off any smoke alarms."

"Yet." A slow smile spread across his face as he pointed to the square box above the door. "Good thing, too, because these smoke alarms are tied into the city fire department."

"Good to know. Anyway, to answer your question— we're off to a good start." With Mindy at the table lending the teens a hand, Sarah turned her back to them and lowered her voice. "Your suggestion about beginning with breakfast was a hit."

"Told you it would be. Teach them the basics and

build up from there. Eggs are one of the simplest things to cook…for most people."

"Hey, I didn't burn that third batch." She struggled not to stick out her tongue.

"You're right. Those had a slightly less charred taste."

"One of these days I'm going to knock your socks off with my cooking, Mr. Seaver."

"I may be on Medicare by the time that happens, Ms. Sullivan." His teasing tone melted away some of her anxiety. She was so afraid he wasn't going to show, and then she'd have been left to her own devices. That was a disaster in the making.

"You scoff at my abilities now, but you'll see… I'm a fast learner." He didn't need to know she'd been poring over cookbooks and watching cooking shows in her spare time. Or see the amount of burned food she'd thrown away, making her bank account cry. At least she hadn't set off any more smoke alarms this past week.

She slipped an apron off the hook by the door and tossed it to him. "Now that you're here, suit up. You can help us with the next step."

He caught the apron with his left hand, but his mouth tightened and his nostrils flared. His eyes darted around the room. A ragged breath squeezed from his chest. Color drained from his face.

She cocked her head and frowned. "You okay?"

"Hey, Miss Sarah, who's the dude? Your boyfriend?" Garrett winked and nudged his buddy.

"No, Garrett, he's my…friend who will be helping us with cooking this summer." Sarah reached for Alec's arm and tried to pull him deeper into the kitchen, but he stood his ground. He stiffened and shook off her hand while taking a step back.

Was she jumping to conclusions with that last identifier?

She and Alec were friends, weren't they? Over the past week of cooking lessons, they'd developed a sort of rapport. His growling lessened in the kitchen, so that was good, right?

"Well, your friend's about to split."

Sarah turned to find Alec stalking to the door. "Excuse me a minute, guys." She left the kitchen and hurried after him. "Alec, wait up. Alec."

Alec ignored her call, flung the door open and let it slam behind him without even turning around.

What in the world had gotten into him?

She couldn't exactly chase after him. She had a responsibility to the teens, especially with that same charred-egg smell she'd come to recognize filtering through the air. With a shrug and an eye roll, she sauntered into the kitchen as if she didn't care about Alec's actions. But her insides swirled like those beaten eggs. What had caused him to bolt? Was it something she'd said?

Alec pushed through the community center door and gulped large mouthfuls of air. He grasped the metal railing with a trembling hand and forced his shallow breathing to stabilize. A gust of wind pummeled his face, cooling the sweat on his brow and upper lip.

What was he doing? He must've been out of his mind to agree to help Sarah with this program. He couldn't work with kids. He should've just texted her and canceled for today, promising to make it up to her. But, no, Mr. Man-of-his-Word showed up and then hightailed it out of there faster than his sister being chased by a snake.

He was such an idiot.

What kind of guy let a group of teenagers get under his skin? They were a bunch of kids. Harmless, right? He'd thought the same thing about Justin, too.

But that didn't make it right to walk out on Sarah, especially since she's been putting in time every day since their agreement at his uncle's house, making a dent in the mess. She did have great organizational skills. And now he wasn't living up to his end of the bargain.

He sat on the steps and buried his face in his hands. This day couldn't end fast enough.

After the housing deal he'd been working on fell through and the irate owners and their screaming toddler caused him to show up late at the community center, he knew he wasn't in the right frame of mind to spend the next two hours in the kitchen.

Apparently Sarah had everything under control anyway. No smoke alarms had gone off, and the kitchen still appeared intact. She didn't need him. And he didn't need to spend the next hour calming down from the panic attack that threatened to squeeze the breath from his chest. Yet here he was.

Behind him, the community center door opened.

"Alec."

He glanced over his shoulder at Sarah standing a few steps behind him, then dropped his gaze to focus on the intricate pattern stamped into the concrete steps.

He wasn't in the mood for a lecture, and he was sure she was ready to blast him about walking out on her.

She laid a hand on his shoulder. "You okay?"

"Yeah." He pushed out a ragged breath.

"Was it something I said? Or did?"

He hated the hesitancy in her voice…and knowing he was the cause of it.

"No, it's nothing you did. I just…" How could he explain himself to her when even he wasn't quite sure what had him running for the door? What else could he say? A bunch of teenagers turned him into a first-class wuss? Grown men shouldn't be having panic attacks.

Alec fixated on a daisy growing in the crack in the sidewalk. Despite the hard circumstances and daily foot traffic, the flower thrived in the sunshine. It reminded him of Sarah. She deserved some sort of explanation.

"Four years ago, I worked for the fire department. We volunteered in our off-hours as mentors to at-risk kids in the community."

"That's a noble thing to do."

"No more than what you're doing." And he meant it. Anyone who could do her job deserved a prize.

"What happened?" She sat on the step next to him, close enough for him to smell her shampoo. The edge of her pink skirt brushed the tops of her knees.

"Shouldn't you be inside?" He jerked a thumb over his shoulder toward the door. Why had he begun this conversation?

"Mindy's in there. Plus, Pastor Nate walked over from the church and they're holding down the fort for a few minutes."

Great. He hadn't seen the volunteers in the kitchen. Someone else to witness his freak-out.

"What happened with the program?" The soft, questioning tone of her voice frayed the already ragged edges of his nerves.

He shrugged. "Nothing. As far as I know, they're still doing it."

"What changed, then?"

"A kid named Justin. His dad was an alcoholic—a mean drunk at that. Justin and I bonded over music, and

I was teaching him how to play guitar. Things seemed to be going well until he came to me with a black eye. I had to report it."

"Of course. His safety was your first priority."

"One would think. Somehow he found out I gave the anonymous tip about the same time his mom, desperate to escape her abusive husband, set their house on fire while Justin's dad was passed out inside."

"Oh, no!"

"We arrived on the scene in time to put the fire out. Justin's dad ended up in the ICU, and his mom was arrested. Justin blamed me. I tried to get him to calm down and promised him everything would be okay. Biggest mistake of my life." Alec rubbed a finger and thumb over his eyes. "He and his brother were put in emergency foster care. He promised I'd pay for destroying his family."

"What happened?"

"We were on scene at another incident when a call came in for a residential fire. 731 Meadowbrook Drive."

"You remember the address?"

"Yes. I'll never forget it. It was my house." He struggled to breathe, the memory still as fresh as when it happened four years ago. "Where I lived with my pregnant wife of almost two years."

Sarah sucked in a sharp breath.

"The fire consumed our house quickly. I tried to save her." Unbidden tears pricked his eyes. "The fire. It was too hot. I did everything I could. But…" His chest tightened. "I lost everything that night because I got involved in a troubled kid's life, hoping to make a difference. I can't afford to make the same mistake twice."

Sarah stood, her expression torn. "Alec, I had no idea. Why did you even agree to working with me?"

"I don't know. I needed help with Emmett's house. If I did this for you, then I could use your assistance without feeling guilty about it. Plus…" He shrugged. "I thought maybe enough time had passed to where I could handle it again. When I walked into that kitchen…"

"It came rushing back?"

"Something like that."

"Have you talked to anyone?"

"Like who? About what?"

"Like someone who specializes in PTSD."

"You think I have post-traumatic stress disorder?"

She lifted a shoulder. "I don't know. Maybe. Panic attacks. Lack of sleep. A couple of common signs."

"I'm fine."

"Okay, then, if you're fine, let's head back inside."

Alec hesitated. He *was* fine. Other than the night-mares that jerked him away from time to time, and the scent of smoke that made him want to crawl out of his skin, he was golden.

But to go back inside?

The group assembled in the kitchen, focused on breaking eggs, looked like a bunch of regular kids, not disturbed pyromaniacs out for revenge. But how could Sarah look at them and see promise? All he saw was potential destruction. Was there really any hope in help-ing them?

Justin could've been any one of those kids. He'd shown promise, needing someone to believe in him. Someone to help him see he could do great things. Alec had tried, and it cost him everything.

How could he risk that again?

But then again, he had nothing left to lose.

A slight throat clearing jerked him out of his thoughts. He blinked a couple of times and caught Sarah's pointed look and raised eyebrow. She stood over him and extended a hand to help him to stand.

If only it were that simple.

Something Billy, his brother-in-law, had asked prodded at his brain… Would Christy want to see him living this way?

He was left with one giant choice—face his fears or let a bunch of kids send him running for the door. Neither option sounded appealing, but he couldn't continue down the path he'd been walking.

He put his hand in Sarah's and forced his legs to move. Steeling his spine and squaring his shoulders, he spoke with more bravado than he felt. "Let's do this."

Hopefully history wouldn't repeat itself.

Chapter Five

Well, he'd managed to last the week without falling apart or hurting anyone. He deserved a medal or something, didn't he? Or at least a quiet weekend without answering anyone's demands. Other than a house showing first thing in the morning, he had the rest of the weekend to himself.

Putting up a tough front was draining.

From out on the community center's front steps, Sarah's laughter swirled through the open door and tugged at his heart. She did a fist bump with one of Amber's little brothers. She definitely had a way with these kids. They respected her, which had made the week a bit more bearable. He admired that, yet a sense of caution continued to stay at the forefront of his mind. He wasn't about to let his guard down.

"Yo, Mr. S. You got a minute?" A hesitant voice spoke behind him.

Alec turned away from watching Sarah to find Daniel standing in the community center kitchen doorway. With neatly trimmed blond hair, a shoulder pressed to the doorjamb and a thumb hooked through the belt loop of his baggy cargo shorts, the kid didn't appear to pose a threat.

"What's up?" Alec crossed his arms over his chest and pressed his back against the stainless-steel industrial-sized deep sink.

The fifteen-year-old shifted his gaze to the outdated linoleum, then looked at Alec with eyes full of curiosity and…a touch of vulnerability. His neck reddened. "I was wondering… I mean…well, how did you get to be a good cook?"

Alec dropped his eyes to the menus he and Sarah had been working on for next week. "I didn't really have a choice. I lost my dad when I was fifteen. He was a marine and was killed by friendly fire."

"Whoa."

"Yeah."

"That's tough, man."

Alec slipped his hands in his front pockets. "It was. After Dad's funeral, I realized I needed to take care of my mom and little sister. We could eat PB&J only so long…know what I mean?"

Daniel laughed softly and stepped into the room, his eyes serious and tone sobering. "Yeah, I do. My parents were killed in a crash over Christmas. My kid brother, Toby, and I live with my grandma. She's tired after working all day and not in the best of health. I feel like it's up to me to be the man of the house, I guess."

Oh, man.

Something inside Alec shifted as he looked at the quiet kid who he'd seen treat others with respect but keep to himself. "I'm sorry for your loss." Alec crossed the room and set a hand on the kid's bony shoulder. "How are you doing?"

Daniel shrugged and looked off into the distance.

"Okay. We left Pittsburgh and moved to Shelby Lake to live with Gram." His eyes filled and his chin trembled. Clenching his jaw, he sniffed and ran a hand under his nose. "My dad and I went to Pirates games and stuff. Mom made these great pierogies. She promised to teach me someday…" His voice trailed off as he sniffed again. "I miss our house, my friends, the cool places to grab a bite."

Alec gave his shoulder a gentle squeeze, then shoved his hand back into his pocket. "I get it, man. I do. My dad was stationed in California when he was killed. Coming to Shelby Lake was a bit of a change, but in time, this place grew on me. Now it's home. Give it a chance."

"I know, and I'm trying." Daniel kicked at the linoleum with the toe of his sneaker. "So what advice can you give me to become a better cook so I can help out Gram?"

Alec admired the kid's integrity, but a warning sounded inside his head. Hadn't Justin come to him all quiet and respectful? They had bonded over their love of music. Alec pushed those thoughts away and looked at Daniel.

Sadness glazed the kid's eyes. Had he laughed once this week? Hung out with the other kids? Acted like an idiot with the rest of them? Alec's thoughts tumbled through the mental pictures of the past few days. No, not once did he remember Daniel becoming part of the group. He kept his distance.

Something Alec knew all too well. He didn't want to bond with the kid, but Daniel did seek him out for advice. The least he could do was steer him in the right direction. He could still keep his distance and protect himself.

Alec waved a hand over the kitchen, "Honestly, Daniel, if you stay in the outreach program, then you're going to learn a lot. Sarah's doing a great job teaching you guys about simple meal planning, shopping on a budget and making food that doesn't come from a box."

The corner of Daniel's mouth tipped up. "I think Miss Sarah's learning the cooking part along with the rest of us. She said she set off the smoke alarm making popcorn."

Alec's mouth twitched. He knew all too well. "She's a quick learner and holds her own."

"She's pretty great."

Alec nodded, then froze. What was he doing? So maybe he respected Sarah's talents in connecting with the teens and appreciated her ability to learn quickly, but that didn't mean he thought she was pretty great.

Sarah called from the open front entrance. "Daniel, your gram's here."

"Okay, just a sec." He turned back to Alec and held out a hand. "Thanks, man."

Alec shook his hand, then clapped him on the shoulder again. "No problem."

Alone in the kitchen, Alec gathered the dirty towels and dishcloths. He'd take them home and wash them. One less thing for Sarah to do.

They shared the same amount of hours, but the stuff she managed to get done amazed him.

After leaving the center, she spent a couple of hours at his uncle's house, packing, tossing and organizing. Alec stopped in when he didn't have evening appointments, but he had to admit he was little help. Sarah claimed it was because he had an emotional attachment to the house and everything in it. She was probably right.

The door slammed closed as his phone chimed in his pocket. He fished it out to find Kathy, Uncle Emmett's home health nurse, calling.

"Alec Seaver," he answered as Sarah breezed into the kitchen, her wildflower scent following her like a shadow.

The older woman's voice sounded hesitant. "Alec, I'm sorry to bother you, but I'm concerned about Emmett."

"What's wrong?" Alec gripped the phone, his gut tightening.

"Well, if you ask him, everything's fine, but he's not socializing and I'm afraid he's becoming depressed. Plus, he fired me again."

"I'm sorry. That's the third time since he moved in." Alec's shoulders dropped, thankful her concern wasn't dire. "I can head over there now and talk to him."

"It doesn't have to be immediately. I don't want to pull you away from your work."

"Family first, Kathy. Besides, I'm done for the day." He ended the call, gathered the bag of towels and brushed past Sarah for the front door.

"I need to go see Emmett."

Sarah's flip-flops slapped against the linoleum as she caught up with him and fell in step, concern lining her face. "Everything okay?"

Alec repeated his conversation with Kathy. "I'm going to talk to him."

"Want some company?"

"You don't need to get caught up in my problems."

"I understand depression." A shadow crossed her eyes, but she smiled so quickly he wondered if he'd imagined it. "Maybe I can help."

Alec looked at her a moment. How would Little Miss

Sunshine know about depression? Working with youth? Or something personal? "Fine, but you'll have to excuse Emmett's cranky demeanor."

"Nothing I haven't dealt with before."

"Actually this is good timing. He's been wanting to meet the girl I hired to go 'rooting through his stuff.'" Alec made air quotes around the last phrase.

Sarah's laughter followed him as he crossed the parking lot and slid into the driver's seat. He tossed the bag of towels on the passenger seat, cranked the AC and waited a moment while Sarah unlocked her car and disappeared inside.

They drove separately to the Lakeside Suites. Alec wound his car around the semicircular drive, then parked in the paved lot facing a backyard with a gazebo, fountain, well-maintained flower beds and a boccie court. Sarah parked next to him.

They entered the building, which opened into an open sitting room with large glass windows that bathed the room in sunshine and smelled like lemon oil. Two ladies sat on a couch, chatting over small porcelain teacups. A man read the newspaper.

Alec knocked on Uncle Emmett's apartment door. When he didn't open it, Alec used his key to get inside. The blaring TV greeted them. He strode into the small apartment, picked up the remote off the small side table next to the worn recliner and turned down the volume.

Uncle Emmett stirred, a frown pinching his eyebrows together. "I was watching that."

"You still can, but I'd like to keep my eardrums intact."

"What'd you say?" His gravelly voice lifted.

"Kathy called and said you fired her again."

"I don't need a nurse." Uncle Emmett pulled his

glasses off his face and cleaned them with his white handkerchief. Despite having been retired for over a decade, Emmett continued to dress as if he were heading for the classroom in his white dress shirt and favored bow tie.

"That's what you said the other two times."

"She has cold hands."

"I heard you the first time." Alec kept his tone neutral. Losing his cool wouldn't benefit either of them. Why did his uncle have to be so stubborn?

"Apparently I'm not the one with a hearing problem because you keep sending her back." Uncle Emmett lowered the footrest on his chair and started to stand without reaching for his cane. His legs wobbled, and he would've pitched forward if Alec hadn't reached out to steady him.

Alec guided him back onto the chair. "That's because you need someone to look after you."

The older man shook off Alec's arm and glared at him. With a shaky hand, he rubbed perspiration off his forehead. "I'm doing just fine on my own, thank you."

"No, you aren't. And you know it. Once you stop fighting me on it, then things will go a lot smoother."

"Hmmph. Smoother?" Uncle Emmett's gray, bushy eyebrows puckered. "What's so smooth about a man being kicked out of his own home?"

Not this again.

Alec sighed. "No one kicked you out of your house. You're no longer able to live by yourself. Doctor's orders. Living here allows you to keep your independence, and this way someone will be able to help you when you need it."

"I'll get married again." The petulant tone reminded

Alec of the defiant toddler in his office this morning with the angry sellers.

Alec adjusted the window blinds and allowed sunshine to spill across the beige carpet. "You'd have to leave your apartment to meet someone, don't you think?"

"I'll join one of those online dating sites I've seen advertised on TV."

"You refuse to use a computer. Besides, marriage isn't the answer to your problem, Emmett."

Emmett dropped his chin to his chest and rubbed the dulled gold band on his left hand. "That house was the only thing I had left of my Elsie."

The old man's sadness softened Alec's attitude. He understood his pain. He patted Uncle Emmett's chest near his heart. "Weren't you the one who told me everything was right here?"

"Fine." He leaned back and closed his eyes. A moment later, he opened them and pointed at Sarah. "Who's that?"

Alec had forgotten she was there. She hadn't said a word since they came, and he had gotten caught up with Emmett. "She's my friend—the one's who's helping me organize your house."

He glared at Sarah. "You're the one pawing through my things."

She flashed Emmett a smile Alec had seen her use more than once this past week with the teens—usually when they were about to challenge her and she wouldn't back down. "You have an impressive book collection."

"Not anymore. Now that I've been kicked out of my house, those books will be in boxes and forgotten in some storage unit." He leaned back in his worn recliner once again and closed his eyes.

Sarah crossed the room and sat on the floor by Emmett's chair, drawing her knees to her chest. "Stinks, doesn't it? Leaving your home and everything you love."

"Yes." His eyes shot open and widened with surprise. "Yes, it does."

"I'm sure you're frustrated about having to rely on others."

"What would you know about that?"

"About a year ago, I left my job, my house and everything I loved to move to Shelby Lake, where I knew only a handful of people."

"Why'd you do it?"

A flicker of something shadowed her eyes, but she blinked several times. Maybe Alec had imagined it. "I needed a fresh start. My fiancé ended our engagement six weeks before our wedding. I came to Shelby Lake to help my brother with his daughters and to see what new plan God had for me."

Ouch.

"Sounds like he wasn't the right guy. But you're young—you have your life ahead of you. I'm an old man, sent here to live out my remaining years."

"It's not like that and you know it." Alec tried to stay patient, but were they going to have this conversation every time they were together?

Sarah stood and picked up a framed photo of Emmett and Gideon. "You're welcome to feel that way, Mr. Browne, but it won't change your situation. From what I understand, you're free to come and go as you please. Your son lives down the street, right? Now you can see him more often. Plus, I'm sure if you talk to the other residents, you'll find many of them may have had similar feelings. When we came in, two ladies were talking about a book they just read. A guy was doing the crossword in the paper...in pen. If you give yourself a chance, you can learn to find the joy in your situation."

"How'd you get so smart?"

"The hard way, but no matter my circumstances, God is unchanging and helps me get through what I'm facing."

Emmett looked at her, then at Alec. "You listening to her? She speaks truth, my boy."

"We're not talking about me, Emmett. How about going down to the living room and getting to know a couple of people? Dinner's going to be served soon. Perhaps you could sit in the dining room today instead of eating in your suite? I'll even go with you."

"I don't need a babysitter. I can do things by myself." Emmett gazed out the window, silent for a moment, then lowered the footrest on his recliner. He stood, straightened his bow tie and reached for his wooden cane. "Let's go."

Apparently he wasn't ready to do dinner by himself.

Alec tossed a smile at Sarah, suddenly appreciating her people skills even more. He'd give her a hug if it wouldn't be out of line. Her ability to relate to his uncle's frustration caused Alec's opinion of her to skyrocket. After spending so much time with her the past week, he'd learned she was anything but a scatterbrain.

Sarah touched his arm and beckoned him to come closer. He leaned in enough to inhale the scent of her shampoo. Her breath fanned his ear. "Do you trust me?"

"About what?" He hated the hesitation that crept into his voice, but trusting others didn't come easily these days.

"I have an idea to help your uncle feel more at home, but I need you to have some faith in me...and the key for this apartment."

"What for?"

She dropped her hand on her hip and shot him a saucy grin. "That's where the trust part comes in. And you must keep your uncle busy for a few hours."

Alec narrowed his eyes and searched her face, taking in those high cheekbones and the smattering of freckles across the bridge of her nose. Sighing, he reached into his pocket and folded the key into her hand, allowing his fingers to linger a second longer than necessary to feel the softness of her skin.

He hoped he didn't regret trusting her.

Sarah had no guarantee her plan would work, but she had to try.

The sadness in Emmett's face carved a hole in her heart. She understood starting over, leaving behind almost everything she held dear, but she also found stepping outside her comfort zone offered new opportunities to reach out to others.

Like the teens in her summer outreach program. Like Alec.

If she hadn't moved to Shelby Lake, then she may have never met her cranky landlord, who used his surliness to keep people at arm's length.

Sarah unlocked Emmett's apartment door and held it open so Daniel and Caleb, Sarah's brother, could carry in one of the bookcases from Emmett's house. Alec had said it was one of his favorites, given to him upon his retirement from teaching English for forty years at Shelby Lake High School. Behind them, Toby followed with a box of classics with worn spines and ragged edges to line the shelves.

For the next thirty minutes, they hauled in a few pieces of furniture. Even if they weren't his favorites, they could be swapped out for ones of his choosing. The point was to make the suite feel more like home.

When she'd arrived earlier in the afternoon with Alec, she hadn't expected such sparse furnishings, especially given Emmett's penchant for holding on to memories. She totally understood needing to downsize, but it was as if the poor guy didn't have any memories in his new place. She hoped to fix that.

Sarah arranged a couple of silver-framed photos of family on the side table next to Emmett's recliner. She included a lamp from the living room and set out a jigsaw puzzle on the small oval table Caleb had pulled out of the kitchen.

Daniel and Toby removed records in their original jackets from a box and slid them into place beneath the outdated, but well-used, stereo with turntable.

She pulled her phone from her back pocket and thumbed through it to find the picture she'd snapped of his home's living room the first day she'd seen it. Then, she instructed Caleb and Daniel where to position the couch. She arranged the needlepoint pillows and tossed the knitted afghan across the back cushions. It took up a large chunk of the living room, but seeing the one worn cushion made Sarah think it had been used quite often.

Another glance at her phone showed they had less than ten minutes left. Alec had agreed to keep Emmett out for two hours. He said he'd take Emmett to Jacob House to see Gideon after dinner. Working quickly, they finished turning Emmett's sparsely decorated suite into some semblance of his former home…without the clutter.

Maybe he'd hate it, and she'd need the guys to help her haul everything back to his house, but something told her Emmett was a man steeped in tradition…someone who thrived on routine.

So much like Alec.

Her phone chimed. A text from Alec.

E's getting tired. We're heading back.

All's well here, she texted back.

Minutes later, she heard voices in the hall. Caleb gave her a quick hug, then he and the boys slipped through the sliding glass door that led out onto a small patio. Sarah hurried to the door and threw it open, meeting Emmett's startled expression.

"Young lady, what are you still doing in my apartment?"

Sarah reached for his free hand, giving his sausage fingers a gentle squeeze. "Mr. Browne, we met for the first time today, but I've gotten to know you a little as I've been organizing your home. Please know I hold the deepest respect for your privacy. As I said earlier, I also understand how you may be feeling." She paused and drew in a deep breath, then released it in a nervous huff. "While you and Alec were out, I wanted to try to blend some of the familiar with the new, but if you don't like it, I will put everything back the way it was."

Emmett glanced at Alec and jerked his head toward Sarah. "She always talk this fast?"

Alec smirked and nodded. "Yes, pretty much."

"Makes a man's ears tired."

Sarah tried not to let his words wound her. She only wanted to help, to lift the sag in his shoulders. Maybe this was a mistake. Maybe she'd intruded without invitation.

Emmett cleared his throat. "Young lady, are you

going to stand guard in front of my door or may I go in and rest my bones?"

"Sorry." Sarah stepped aside and released the door handle. "Just remember what I said."

Emmett frowned and grunted, pushing the door open.

Her heart picked up speed. She wiped her damp hands on her shorts.

Frank Sinatra crooned from the turntable, filling the room with his velvety voice.

Thank you, Daniel, for that last touch.

Emmett shuffled into the living room, then stopped, leaning heavily on his cane. He turned slowly, his gaze lingering on his wedding photo that Sarah had found stacked on the table and hung up where he could see it from his favorite recliner. He moved to the couch and ran a shaky hand across the afghan that lay over the back. He tightened his grip on his cane as he lowered himself onto a cushion. Patting his breast pocket, he reached for a white handkerchief.

He shifted watery eyes to Alec. "You knew about this?"

"Not exactly. Sarah asked me to trust her."

Sarah moved to the couch and rested a hand on the older man's shoulder. "Mr. Browne, I apologize if I've intruded on your space…" Her voice trailed off as Emmett's gaze slid around the room.

Steadying himself on his cane, he rose. He moved from the couch to the bookcase to the table, taking in everything without saying a word. He trailed a finger down the spine of one of the books and sniffed. Then sniffed again.

Standing in front of his wedding photo, he lowered his head, pinning his chin to his chest.

Pressure mounted behind Sarah's eyes as her shoulders sagged. She kept her eyes glued to her flip-flops. The last thing she'd wanted was to upset the man. She shot a quick look at Alec, who stood behind Emmett with a scowl creasing his forehead. He wrapped an arm around the elderly man's shoulders.

Great. What a way to win friends.

"Unc—"

"Mr. Browne—"

They spoke in unison. Sarah snapped her mouth closed and stepped back. She put her hands behind her back and turned to stare out the window.

Behind her, the men spoke in hushed tones. She couldn't stand it any longer. Reaching into her pocket, she pulled out Alec's key. She walked over to him and held it out. "Listen, I'm really sorry about this. I just wanted to help. I'll have Caleb come back and we'll get everything back where it belongs."

Emmett stepped between her and Alec. Giving his eyes a final swipe, he looked at her with a gentle smile brightening his face. "Young lady, you will do no such thing. This is one of the nicest things anyone's done for me. I appreciate the time you took to make an old man feel at home."

The knots in her stomach loosened as her fingers around his suite key relaxed. She pressed a kiss against his wrinkled cheek, then stepped back, returning the smile. "I was very happy to help. Now, if you'll excuse me, I need to be going." Nodding to the men, she picked up her purse and hurried for the front door.

"Sarah!"

She stopped in the hall, the loose knots in her stomach tightening again. Was he coming to yell at her for overstepping her bounds? Only one way to find out.

She turned to find Alec striding toward her. He stopped in front her with a bemused expression on his face. "Forgetting something?"

She frowned. "I don't think so."

"Emmett's key?"

"Oh! That's right. Emmett stepped between us before you could take it. Sorry about that. And listen—I apologize if I stuck my nose in where it didn't belong. It's just that…well…the look on that poor man's face just got to me. That's all." She let out a sigh and waited for a response, and she handed him the key.

Instead of speaking, Alec's eyes searched her face. What was he thinking?

He took the key from her, but instead of pocketing it, he gave her hand a gentle tug, catching her off guard. She stumbled toward him and placed her palms against his chest to keep from falling. His heart pounded against her hand.

He gripped her arms gently, then gathered her against his chest. Wrapping his arms around her, he leaned down and whispered, his breath warming her ear, "You did an incredibly sweet thing for Uncle Emmett."

Sarah should've pushed away, but she liked the feel of his strong arms around her. The scent of his cologne tangled in the threads of his button-down shirt, and the rhythmic beating of his heart seeped through her, patching cracks and empty spaces in her heart.

She needed to get a grip. It was only a hug of gratitude. Nothing more.

But, deep down, if she cared to admit her true feelings, she'd confess the hug felt like more…at least, to her.

And she wasn't quite sure how to handle that. She

wasn't going to allow herself to fall for her landlord.
A man who was battling his own issues. Somehow,
though, she needed to convince her heart of that decision.

Chapter Six

Sarah's decision wasn't going to make Alec happy. And he had a valid reason for not wanting to get involved with teens again, but what choice did she have? Surely she could get him to see reason. Besides, it was only for the night. So where was the harm in that?

But she couldn't shake the vulnerability she'd seen in his eyes that first day of the program when he'd shared his past. Maybe it would be all right as long as she kept the boys away from him. And they were such good kids, too. Definitely not troublemakers.

Sarah sat in the bentwood rocker in Daniel and Toby's living room and dug her bare toes into the beige carpet. Despite the hand-stitched quilt thrown over the back of the chair, she could feel the holes in the caning.

Screams and laughter from the other kids in the mobile-home park filtered in through the open window. She'd have to remember to close it once the boys were done gathering their things, but for now it cleared the stuffy air tinged with humidity, canned air freshener and despair.

Family photos in dollar-store frames hung on the paneled wall above the worn flowered couch with wooden arms. Embroidered throw pillows reminded her of the ones she'd seen at Alec's uncle's house. A laptop sat on a scarred end table next to the couch.

Her heart went out to Nancy, the boys' grandma. She was doing the best she could on her limited income. After losing her daughter and son-in-law at Christmas, she'd been trying to make ends meet for them while waitressing—that is, until the restaurant where she'd worked closed.

Judging by the worn, outdated furnishings and Toby's shirts and shorts that appeared to be a size too small, money wasn't stretching very far.

Daniel and Toby came into the living room with bulging backpacks slung over their shoulders. Daniel reached behind the couch, unplugged the cord and stuffed the computer into his backpack. "We're ready."

Sarah closed the windows, followed the boys outside and waited while Daniel locked the front door.

Less than ten minutes later, Sarah pulled into her driveway. Her heart sank. The open garage door revealed Alec's luxury sedan parked in the left bay. Even though she couldn't see him, he couldn't be too far away.

Maybe they could make a mad dash for the apartment without him catching them. But she wasn't doing anything wrong. Not really.

She shut off the ignition and dropped her keys in her purse. Tossing a smile at the boys, she jerked her head toward the house. "Come on, guys. I'll give you the fifty-cent tour."

They scrambled out of the car, grabbed their backpacks and followed her to the porch. She reached her door about the same time as Alec's opened and he stepped outside.

Dressed in khaki cargo shorts and a navy T-shirt, he nodded at her and flashed a quick smile. But the moment he caught sight of the boys, the smile disappeared under the weight of his puckered brows. Lines bracketed his thin lips.

Sarah smiled. "Hey, Alec. You remember Daniel and Toby, right? From the summer outreach program?"

Nodding, Alec thrust his hands in his pockets. "Boys."

"Mr. Seaver." Daniel lifted a hand in greeting.

"A word, Sarah?"

"Sure, no problem." She turned and handed Daniel her set of keys. "Hey, guys, give us a minute, will you? Head upstairs and make yourselves at home. There are cold drinks in the fridge. I'll order pizza as soon as I'm done talking with Alec."

Daniel studied them a minute, then reached for the keys. Neither said a word as they took the stairs two at a time. Once they unlocked the door and let themselves inside, she steeled her spine and faced Alec. "What's up?"

With his back pressed against the porch railing, he folded his arms over his chest and crossed his ankles. The intensity of his stare made her want to squirm, but she refused to be intimidated. The boys needed her today, and it *was* only temporary.

Sliding her sunglasses to the top of her head, she kept her tone casual, repeating, "You wanted a word?"

He nodded toward her closed door. "What are they doing here?"

"Their grandma fell off a chair and broke a hip. Daniel called me from the hospital, very upset."

"So why are they here?"

"She's their sole caregiver, so I brought them home with me. With her permission, of course. They're tired, so they're spending the night here to get some rest since I have stuff to do to prep for tomorrow's cooking lesson."

"No."

"No, what?"

"No, the boys aren't staying here." Even though Alec didn't raise his voice, the "my word is final" tone in his voice set her teeth on edge.

Pausing a second to school her tone, she shot him a direct look that showed she refused to back down. "Yes, they are. They have nowhere else to go. They're minors."

"What about CYS?"

She tossed her arms up. "Children and Youth? Seriously? Where's your heart?"

Alec's eyes narrowed. "Your lease states no one else is allowed to live here without prior permission from the landlord, which is me, in case you've forgotten."

"Of course not, but you're being a little ridiculous, don't you think?"

"My house, my rules."

"Wow, total high-school flashback. Have some compassion, Alec. It's not like I tried to sneak them in or anything. Those boys have gone through a lot. They lost both parents in a car accident over Christmas and left everything they knew to move up here to Shelby Lake to live with their grandma. Nancy's been working hard to help them adjust. They're good kids. They've been a part of our church's youth group since they've moved here. They need someone they can trust, and that's me."

She touched his arm. He tensed. Sarah dropped her hand to her side. "Listen, I know you dislike teenagers, but they are good boys, and it's only for tonight. Tomorrow we'll know more about what's going on with Nancy.

Then, if need be, I'll stay at their place until she comes home. Or if it really stresses you out that much, I'll grab a few things and then head back to their place tonight."

Alec ground his jaw and looked over her shoulder. Even though he hadn't changed positions, he remained totally wound. "I don't like it."

"I didn't ask you to. They're teenagers, Alec—not toddlers. They're old enough not to cause any trouble. You didn't seem to mind when Ella and Ava spent the night with me last weekend."

"It's not the same. Little kids like your nieces at least are still learning right from wrong. Teenagers *choose* right from wrong."

"Daniel is a straight-A student. He bags groceries after school to save for college and to help his grandma. Toby is one of the sweetest kids I've met. Since they've moved here, they've come to trust me, and I won't turn my back on them."

Was it only a couple of days since Alec had hugged her after she'd helped his uncle? She'd really thought their relationship had turned a corner and the teens were growing on him. She was a fool for thinking he'd changed.

Instead, he was acting like a jerk.

With her head throbbing and stomach growling, she pushed past him.

Alec reached out and grabbed her elbow. "Sarah, wait."

She stopped, but she didn't turn around, needing a second to temper the words scalding her tongue.

After a moment, Alec pushed away from the railing and moved in front of her, holding up a hand. "Listen, I'm sorry—I overreacted."

At least they agreed on something. "Ya think?"

He ignored her jab. "Do you know what it's like to lose everything?"

"Yes, I do. Even though I haven't experienced the tragedies you've endured, I do know the ache of having your life changed. I refuse to live life in a bubble, afraid of getting hurt again. I'm really sorry about what you've gone through, but you can't paint all teenagers with the same brush. I lost my best friend in high school, but I still create friendships. I had my heart broken, but that doesn't mean I've given up on getting married someday."

Alec headed for his apartment. With his hand on the doorknob, he turned and gave her a long look. "Be careful. Don't be too trusting. I'd hate for you to get hurt."

She watched him disappear into his house. The man confused her, running hot and cold. Half the time he seemed as though he barely tolerated her presence, but then he said things like not wanting to see her get hurt. Didn't he realize he was the one she needed to be careful around? The way her heart pounded and her stomach fluttered when he was around proved he had the potential to hurt her more than anyone else.

Flames shot through the grate, lapping the sizzling meat. Alec painted the chicken breasts with his homemade barbecue sauce. The rich honey-vinegar mixture made his mouth water and stomach growl.

He speared the chicken with more force than necessary and scowled when a chunk of meat fell between the grate into the coals. Great—he'd overcooked it. Within seconds flames devoured the piece, charring it beyond recognition. That's how he felt—burned, charred and definitely scarred.

Shaking away the feeling of bleakness that had crept

over him since his argument with Sarah last night, he carried the platter of poultry through the sliding glass patio door into the kitchen.

After spending the past fifteen minutes in the heat of the afternoon over a hot grill, the cool, air-conditioned room was welcome relief. He set the platter on the table and headed for the sink.

Gran stood at the stove, humming to herself. He recognized the melody as a hymn she sang often, one that talked of God's love, rich and pure.

For as long as he could remember, she'd played the piano at the Shelby Lake Community Church. When he was a little kid, visiting during the summer, he'd sat beside her while she practiced on Saturday mornings. His feet swinging beneath the bench.

Gran would hum as her fingers played the notes. Before long, he was copying her movements. As he grew older, he was one of those odd kids who actually enjoyed piano lessons. Then, in high school, he'd picked up the guitar.

As a child, he spent hours sitting on the floor in Gran and Granddad's den leafing through their old hymnal collection. Granddad would patiently explain the history behind the lyrics and music.

Alec had thought Granddad knew everything. Nowadays, when he visited him in the nursing home, Granddad didn't even know Alec's name. He could blame the Alzheimer's destroying his memory for that.

He washed and dried his hands, then ran a wet paper towel over his heated face. "Gran, why so much chicken? Expecting an army?"

The doorbell rang.

Gran stopped humming. "Get that, would you, honey?"

She dropped a shucked ear of corn into a pot of boiling water.

Alec tossed the paper towel into the trash can and headed for the foyer. Opening the heavy oak door, he stared at Sarah, Daniel and Toby standing on the front porch.

He hadn't seen them since yesterday. What were they doing here?

Sarah wore a green sundress that complemented her eyes and gave her skin a healthy glow. He scowled. He didn't care what she wore or how she looked. Finding his voice, he asked, "May I help you?"

Sarah flashed him a bright smile as if her anger from yesterday had been a figment of his imagination. "You could let us in. We've been invited for dinner."

Gran joined him, drying her hands on a dish towel. "Alec, who's at the door?" Spying her guests, she edged in front of him and smiled. "Sarah. Boys. Come in, come in. Alec, where are your manners? Step back and give them some room."

Alec jerked his head toward the kitchen. "Gran, may I talk to you a moment?"

Gran ignored his request and turned back to her guests, ushering them into the house. "Come in. No need to stand outside in this sweltering heat."

"Thanks for having us." Sarah lifted her nose. "Something smells great."

As Sarah sauntered past, he caught a whiff of her perfume. He really had to stop paying attention to that.

Gran showed them to the living room. "Make yourselves comfortable. I'll be right with you."

As soon as Sarah and the boys were settled, Gran grabbed Alec by the arm and pulled him to the kitchen. Even though he was a good foot taller and outweighed her by at least fifty pounds, he felt six years old all over again.

Once the door swung closed behind them, Alec faced Gran. "You invited them for dinner?" At Gran's nod, he continued. "Why didn't you say something earlier?"

"Why does it matter?" Her voice remained calm, almost placating.

"It does to me."

Gran's eyes narrowed. "Give me a good reason why Sarah and those boys shouldn't be here, and I'll ask them to leave. Sarah has her hands full with the outreach program and all the work she's been doing at Emmett's. Now she's helping out Nancy—who happens to be a friend, by the way—by caring for those boys. I figured inviting them to dinner was the least I could do. If you don't care to eat with us, then you're welcome to leave."

He stared. "You're kicking out your own grandson?"

Gran shook her head. "No, I'm giving you a choice. You're always welcome here. If you want to stay for dinner, that's fine, too, but you won't be rude to my guests. Those boys are going through a tough time right now. Get to know them. You'll see they're nothing like Justin. Stop letting your past cloud your judgment, young man."

Alec held up his hands. "Let's not get into that again."

Young man.

Those boys in the living room were young men. Not him. Not anymore. Haggard and worn-out, he felt every one of his thirty-two years. He spun around one of the kitchen chairs and straddled it. A dull ache thumped at his temples. He rubbed his forehead.

Gran moved behind him and placed her hands on his shoulders, squeezing gently. "You don't have to like them being here, but you won't be rude, either. You know, Alec, our family has had its share of tragedies, but we managed to get through them with God's help. Maybe it's time you asked Him for guidance."

Alec snorted. "Ask God? Right. He's not interested in me."

The light in Gran's eyes dimmed. "Oh, honey, that buried hostility will eat at you like a cancer if you don't let it out. You need to talk to someone."

"I'm fine."

Gran sandwiched his hands between hers. Soft, wrinkled, age-spotted hands that had comforted him more times than he could remember. He shifted his gaze from her hands to her face. Her faded blue eyes stared back at him. If he'd expected to find sympathy, he would have been disappointed. She was one of the most compassionate people he knew, but at the moment she glared at him with the same no-nonsense look she gave him when he was in trouble.

"You're not fine. Until you can admit that, you won't heal or be able to move on with your life. It's time for you to stop wallowing in self-pity and start living again. Now, I need to take care of my guests. You do as you see fit." She left the kitchen and headed to the living room.

Gran's reprimand stung. She didn't know what she was talking about. So he'd quit going to church. Big deal. The hurt he saw in Gran's eyes every time she invited him to go with her left him feeling smaller than a snail's belly, but she didn't understand.

God played favorites when it came to answering prayers. Apparently Alec hadn't been on the A-list, and he wasn't about to set himself up for disappointment again.

Hearing a sudden burst of laughter erupt behind the kitchen door, loneliness stole over him.

He dealt with people on a daily basis and prided himself on having the social skills to handle difficult clients. Daniel and Toby hadn't done anything to earn his skepticism, and honestly, they were pretty decent kids. So why was he stalling in the kitchen?

He had two choices—grab something on the way home to eat by himself in front of the TV or man up and enjoy Gran's cooking. His stomach grumbled again, solving the problem for him.

Taking a deep breath, he hefted the platter of chicken with one hand, a chilled bowl of pasta salad with another and turned to find Sarah standing in the kitchen doorway with her arms folded over her chest. "I'm sorry the invitation caught you by surprise."

He swallowed a sigh. He didn't want to go another round with her. His eyes scanned the counter. Where was his white flag? "No big deal."

"Apparently it is if you're hiding in the kitchen." Her eyes held the same determined look he'd seen yesterday when she came to the boys' defense. "Look, if it's a problem, the boys and I will leave. I don't want to make you uncomfortable."

"Forget it. It's fine."

"The boys are stressed already, Alec. They don't need your attitude. If you can't say anything nice, then just—" She looked as if she wanted to tell him to keep his mouth shut, but she paused, drew a breath, clamped her lips and closed her eyes. Seconds later, she met his gaze with a calmer expression than she'd had moments ago and hugged a quiet breath. "Please don't say anything at all."

Before Alec could reply, the kitchen door flew open

again and his sister, Chloe, burst into the room, her dark, wavy hair pulled back into a ponytail. "Hey, Alec, what's taking you so long? We're starving." Seeing Sarah, she smiled and moved over to hug her. "Hey, Sarah. Great to see you. Charming my big brother, I see."

Sarah returned the hug. "I doubt I'm qualified to do that. He's teaching me to cook."

Chloe's eyes volleyed between the two of them, then she grinned. "I heard about that. He needs something interesting to shake up his dull life."

"I'm right here. Stop talking about me like I'm not." Why did he have this sudden need to explain himself? It wasn't as though he was trying to impress anyone.

"Did I mention he's a bit testy?"

Sarah smirked. "No need. I learned that on my own."

Chloe shot Sarah a saucy wink as she reached for the platter of chicken still balanced on Alec's palm. "I'll carry this to the table so you two can finish the conversation you were having before I butted in. Word of warning, though—if you don't hurry, I'm going to beg Gran to start without you."

"You're great at butting in. Tell Gran we'll be out in a minute, Tink."

Chloe stuck her tongue out at him. "Don't call me that. You know I hate it."

Amusement tugged at the corners of his mouth. "Exactly."

She rolled her eyes and headed for the dining room, muttering under her breath. "Brothers."

Alec thrust the bowl of pasta salad at Sarah. "Make yourself useful. Please," he added as an afterthought.

"We're not finished with this conversation." She

jerked the bowl out of his hands and grabbed the basket of rolls off the table.

Alec bit back the words that formed on his tongue and reached for the steaming corn. The food was going to be cold if they wasted more time. "For now, we are. I'm tired and hungry."

And he needed time to suit up if they were going into battle again.

Chapter Seven

Alec didn't want them here. His attitude couldn't have been clearer. Maybe he felt they had intruded in his private life.

Sarah caught him glaring at her. Again. She glanced around the round oak dining room table, but Gran and Chloe seemed oblivious to the undercurrent of tension that flowed between Sarah and Alec like a live wire. If only she could ignore him.

To be fair, he wasn't a complete grouch.

Remembering the smile while he teased his sister had Sarah wanting to see it again. The expression changed his entire face. Instead of growling like a grizzly, he seemed so…nice. His gruff features softened around Gran, too. His hang-up was with the boys being here. Perhaps her, too.

Shifting her thoughts away from Alec, Sarah tried to focus on Toby's description of the fountain at Point State Park in downtown Pittsburgh, but her attention zeroed in on Daniel.

Daniel had been laughing and talking with Gran and Chloe, but he'd clammed up as soon as Alec entered the room. He ate the rest of his meal in silence with his shoulders hunched as if trying to appear invisible. She thought the two of them had gotten along—Alec mentioned Daniel had asked him some cooking-related questions recently, but Daniel had been sullen and withdrawn since last night. Maybe he'd picked up on the tension, too.

Sarah appreciated Gran's and Chloe's efforts to draw him back into their conversation, but her irritation toward Alec rose every time Daniel glanced at him before responding to his sister or grandmother. She understood the anxiety caused by walking around on eggshells, afraid to upset anyone. Daniel needed to be able to speak up without being concerned about how anyone was going to react.

Toby flicked a piece of red onion from the pasta salad onto the side of his plate. It slid off the edge of the plate onto the white lace tablecloth. Sarah nudged him with her elbow and gave him a slight shake of her head.

Chloe leaned over, bringing her hand to the side of her mouth, and whispered loudly, "That's okay, Toby, I can't stand them, either." She made a face similar to Toby's and showed him the small pile on her nearly empty plate.

He grinned and shoved a spiral of pasta in his mouth.

Suddenly tired, Sarah stifled a yawn, feeling as energetic as the chicken on her plate. She bit into her ear of corn, now lukewarm from sitting untouched. The delicious food eased the hunger pangs, but it settled like a brick in her stomach.

Sarah had jumped at Gran's dinner invitation. Anything to put off cooking. The boys had dealt with enough for one day without needing to be subjected to her culinary experiments.

Chloe moved her plate away and leaned forward

on the table. "So, Sarah, how's the outreach program going?"

Sarah pushed away her fatigue and smiled at Chloe. She took in the younger woman's petite frame, wavy chestnut hair and blue eyes. Eyes like Alec's. "Going well so far, thanks to your brother. If the teens had to rely on my cooking skills, they'd be doomed."

"Alec's always been willing to help others."

Sarah filed that bit of information away. "Are you still able to help us when we get to the babysitting segment?"

Chloe smiled, reaching for her water glass. "Yes, of course. I'm looking forward to it. Is the church still considering a year-round outreach program? If so, maybe we could set up some sort of babysitting certification program."

She appreciated Chloe's enthusiasm and yearned for the permanent program, but she couldn't afford to get her hopes up. "That's a great idea, but it may be a little premature. The church board won't commit until they see how the summer pilot program is going. Then we'll need to consider moving to a more permanent location. The community center has been great, but if we do a full-time program, we need to find a new place because they're redoing the wiring in September."

"What about the church?"

"We've considered it, but we'd prefer to have a neutral building in the community so people who don't attend church won't feel intimidated by it. One of our core goals is to build those relationships and then draw people into the church."

"Makes sense. Maybe Alec could help you find something. If anyone knows about properties in town, it's him."

Sarah smiled. "I'll keep it in mind."

Chloe snapped her fingers and pointed at her brother. "Wait a minute…what about your building, Alec?"

"What building?" Alec's gazed jerked to his sister. Then, as if trying to cover his surprise, he shoved his plate away and leaned back in his chair, folding his arms across his chest.

Chloe looked at him as though he'd sprouted two heads. "You know…the consignment shop."

"What about it?" He stood and reached for his plate.

"You could—"

"No." He spoke in the same authoritative tone Sarah had heard yesterday when she brought the boys back to her apartment. She had no idea what building they were talking about, but apparently it was enough to upset Alec.

"But it's just—"

Alec's sharp tone cut her off. "Drop it, Chloe."

Frowning, she sighed, slouching in her chair. "I'm just saying—"

Deep lines furrowed his forehead. His glare practically bored a hole through his sister. "And I said to drop it."

Sarah raised an eyebrow at the intense expression on Alec's face. Maybe she and the boys should try to excuse themselves so the family could work this out privately.

"Gran, talk to him. You know it would be ideal." Chloe jumped up from the table and started clearing plates. "Boys, would you like to help me in the kitchen? I have it on good authority that Gran has chocolate cake stashed in there somewhere. Let's take ours out to the garden to eat."

The boys grabbed their plates and followed Chloe.

As soon as the kitchen door swung shut, Sarah folded her hands on the table, snuck a fleeting look at Alec, then turned to Gran, getting the feeling she'd be much more calm about the situation. "I apologize if I'm intruding in on a family matter, but what's the deal with this particular building?"

Gran darted a quick glance at Alec, who stood in front of the dining room window with his back to them. She returned her attention to Sarah. "I own a building downtown, a few doors down from Cuppa Josie's."

"It's a consignment shop?"

"Well, sort of. Alec leased the building to use for his late wife's consignment shop."

Christy's Closet.

Pieces began to fall into place.

No wonder Alec was on the verge of a freak-out. The last time she walked in front of that shop, it appeared closed, but a viable business.

"Honestly, it's not my decision to make anyway." Sarah reached for her nearly empty glass of water.

"Maybe not." Gran stood and rested a hand on the back of her chair. "But I'm sure your opinion holds some weight, especially since you're the one who's going to be spending the most time there."

"Gran…" Alec started to speak, but Gran cut him off.

"What?" She shrugged her narrow shoulders. "Really, Alec, what harm is there in looking at the building? She might not even want it."

Alec's gaze captured Sarah's and held. His eyes narrowed into angry slits. Sarah fought to keep her expression neutral but refused to look away.

After what seemed an eternity, Alec broke eye contact and turned away. He raked long fingers through his hair and hissed out a sigh. "What if she does?"

* * *

Alec's fingers stilled on the keys as the final notes echoed through the room. His shoulders sagged from fatigue. Playing usually relaxed him, but not tonight.

Why couldn't Chloe have left well enough alone? She had no business bringing up the building. And Gran had sided with her. Traitors.

The doorbell rang. Alec stifled a groan. Company was the last thing he wanted. He considered not answering the door. Biting back a sigh, he slid off the bench and padded barefoot through the living room.

A glance through the peephole showed Sarah standing on the other side. He ran a hand over his face. What did she want now?

He opened the door and stood with one hand on the doorknob and the other braced against the doorjamb. "What can I do for you, Ms. Sullivan?"

She slid her fingers through her hair, then gestured toward his open doorway. "May I, uh, come in?"

"I'm really not in the mood for company."

"How about an apology from a friend?"

"An apology for what?"

She lifted a shoulder. "I feel as if you were ambushed about your wife's store."

Okay, so he wasn't expecting that.

Alec hesitated, then stepped back, allowing her to enter. Closing the door, he wavered between inviting her to sit down or keeping her standing in the entryway. Good manners prevailed. He ushered her into the living room.

Sarah remained silent as she wandered around, picking up assorted family photos Chloe had given him, claiming they added warmth to the room. Sarah sat on the leather couch and ran her hand across the wooden coffee table Gran had given him, along with the matching end tables. She glanced at him, then nodded toward his piano. "Your playing was beautiful. You're very talented."

"Thanks."

She firmed her jaw and looked him in the eye. "I'm sorry about what happened at dinner. I wanted to let you know I won't be badgering you to look at the building. For one, I'm not in a place of authority to make that decision, and two, I don't want there to be anything weird between us. You're such a great help with the teens, and I'd hate to lose you."

"Thanks. I appreciate that." Alec rubbed the nape of his neck. "My family's been after me for a couple of years to clean it out."

"I'm sure that must be hard."

"You have no idea." He sat next to her and clasped his hands between his knees, fixating his gaze on a random spot on the beige carpet. "I'm not delusional, you know. I know she's not coming back."

"Maybe it's too overwhelming. Maybe you're uncertain of where to start. Kind of like Emmett's house." The calm, soothing yet questioning tone in her voice reminded him of the couple of times he'd visited a counselor after Christy's death.

"Yes, something like that." He covered his nose and mouth with his hands and exhaled.

Sarah nudged his shoulder with hers. "You're allowed to ask for help, you know."

"Everyone has too much on their plates already."

She reached for a framed photo of his family taken a couple of years ago when his mom had been stateside. "I'm sure they'd make time for you, Alec. We all need someone to lean on."

"That's a bit hypocritical coming from you." He shot her a sideways look.

"Why do you say that?"

"Because of these." Alec traced the skin under her eyes. "Your plate was full with the program, helping me, which by the way proves I can ask for help, and now you're caring for two lost kids. You need to learn to say no before you pass on advice to anyone else."

"Those boys need someone they can trust to care for them."

"I get that, Sarah. I really do." Alec rubbed his palms together, choosing his next words carefully—he wasn't in the mood for another battle. "Ian and Agnes James are licensed emergency foster parents who are amazing with kids of all ages."

"You're reminding me of that because you don't want the boys here." She jumped to her feet and paced on the other side of his coffee table.

He pushed to his feet. "No, I'm saying it because I'm afraid you're taking on too much."

"Thankfully I'm not your problem to worry about."

His chest seized. He sighed and lowered his voice. "I don't want to see you hurt."

She hesitated, drawing in a deep breath and letting it out in a single whoosh as if to gain strength for her next words. "Why do you even care?"

"Because." Alec crossed his arms over his chest. They were straying into territory he wasn't sure he was ready to explore. She needed to go.

Her quick laugh bounced around the too-quiet room. "Good answer, Mr. Articulate."

"Because you…challenge me." He rounded the table to stand in front of her. "My family treats me as if I were one of Gran's delicate teacups. You show compassion, yet you push me to try new things."

The corner of her mouth lifted. "I believe that's one of the nicest things you've said to me."

"You caught me at a weak moment." He smiled to show he was teasing.

"You keep people at arm's length, Alec, but there's a part of you that wants to draw them in. You're afraid, though, and when that battle wages inside you, you lash out and your jerky side emerges."

"We all have our flaws." Alec jammed his hands in his pockets and moved to the window. Anything to put distance between them. "Not everyone has your Pollyanna ideals, okay?"

Sarah crossed the room and joined him at the window, placing her hand on his shoulder. Her gentle touch warmed his skin. "I don't have Pollyanna ideals, but I do believe in giving people a fair chance. I'm asking you to do the same."

Deep inside he knew she was right. And that was part of the struggle.

Chapter Eight

With the bases loaded, Sarah needed a solid hit to bring her team home so they could win the game. Pulling her sunglasses off her face, she wiped the sweat off her forehead with the back of her hand and squinted against the sunshine beating down on the field. The air was thick with humidity. Gray clouds clustered overhead. Rain would cool things off a bit. Sarah took a swig from her water bottle, enjoying the refreshing coolness of the icy liquid.

"Sarah, you're up." Nate stood at the backstop and nodded toward the field.

She capped her water and set it on the dugout bench. Approaching home plate, her eyes connected with Alec's as he crouched into the catcher's position. Knowing he'd be watching tightened the knot in her stomach, but she tried to focus on the field and not on his muscular arms. He'd arrived wearing a red T-shirt advertising his sister's early learning center and gray shorts.

Even though things had been tense between them the past few days, he continued to show up at the community center to share his cooking skills with the teenagers. When one of them asked him to join their team against the other half of the teens in a friendly game of softball, and he'd said yes, she hadn't been able to contain her surprise. All he'd said when she asked about it was "maybe it was time to give them a chance."

Hearing her name being cheered behind her, Sarah donned a batting helmet and took the bat Daniel held out to her. The helmet glued her sweat-soaked hair to her scalp. The scent of grilling hot dogs caused her stomach to roll.

After waking up with a major headache, the last thing she wanted was to play softball, but the boys had been looking forward to playing…and attending the picnic that was to follow.

And now she and Alec played on opposing teams.

Positioning her feet in the dirt, she moved into a batting stance. She wiped her clammy hands on her shorts, then tightened her grip on the aluminum bat. Tuning out the noise, she nodded to the pitcher to let him know she was ready.

One hit. That's all she needed.

He threw the ball underhand. As it came toward her, Sarah swung and missed. The ball thumped into Alec's mitt.

"Strike one!"

She shuffled her feet, lifted the bat into position again.

"Come on, Miss Sarah. You can do it!"

Her stomach rolled again. She wasn't so sure she could do it. She squeezed her eyes shut for a second, then regained her focus on the pitcher. The only thing she cared about was hitting the ball. Then she could go home and lay on the couch with an ice pack over her eyes to dull the throbbing headache.

The pitcher tossed another underhand ball. She swung and missed.

"Strike two!"

Okay, this was getting ridiculous. She didn't want to strike out in front of Alec. Her pride was at stake. Sweat rolled down between her shoulder blades. She tapped the bat against home plate the way she'd seen the pros do it. Tightening her grip, she crouched into position with her bat ready to connect with the ball.

The pitcher stepped forward and tossed the ball. As soon as the ball was within range, she swung hard. Aluminum connected with leather, the momentum reverberating up her arm. Stunned, she stood watching the ball sail across the field. The outfielders ran like jackrabbits to retrieve it.

"Run, Sarah! Go! Go! Go!" Her team screamed behind the backstop.

She snapped out of her daze and dropped her bat. Pumping her arms, she charged for first base. She touched the bag with her toe. A quick glance showed the other team rushing deeper into the outfield, so she continued to second. Hearing cheers and her name called out by her teammates propelled her feet toward third.

Exhilaration pulsed through her. Despite playing softball in high school, she'd never made it past second base.

A stitch pierced her side, and her chest burned. She tagged the bag and slowed until her team's windmilling arms drew her home.

Alec stood at the home plate with his glove open above his head. She had seconds to master this home run. A scurry of activity out of the corner of her eye warned her to head back to third, but she was so close.

Barreling toward home, she pushed herself to move

faster. Her teammates touched home base, creating dust clouds as they ran. Lungs screaming and sweat dripping into her eyes, Sarah kept her eyes fixed on home plate. The toe of her sneaker tagged the plate as Alec caught the ball and jumped forward to tag her.

Her head came up and knocked into his chin as he reached down to touch her arm with the ball. She tripped over his foot and lost her balance, crashing to the ground with a heavy weight pinning her shoulder to the dirt.

A fiery pain set her nerves and muscles aflame, searing her right arm from shoulder to wrist. Tears blurred her vision. Her splintered breathing caught in her chest. The weight lifted quickly, and she rolled onto her back, cradling her arm to her chest. A whimper slid over her lips.

She cinched her eyes closed to block out the blinding sun. She needed to move—to stand, to get her head off home plate, but every time she tried to sit up, the ground spun and the pain kept her pinned to the dirt. Her stomach rolled. Bile burned her throat.

People called her name, but the only voice she homed in on was Alec's. He knelt beside her and placed his hands on her cheeks, thumbing dirt off her skin. "Sarah, I'm so sorry. Are you hurt?"

"My arm." Her voice sounded as dry as the dirt caking her lips. "And my head."

"You hit the ground pretty hard." He reached for her left hand and slid an arm around her shoulders. "Can you stand?"

Leaning on him, she dug her feet into the ground and forced her legs to lift her. The second her right shoulder left the ground, a scream escaped from her throat. Multicolored spots danced in front of her eyes as darkness rushed through her head. Her stomach tossed again.

"Someone call 911!" Alec's shout close to her ears made her cringe.

"I'm on the phone with them now," Nate called out.

Shouting increased the pulsing in her head. She wanted them to hush, but when she opened her mouth to say something, a wave of nausea crashed over her again. She swallowed several times to push the feeling down. Dropping to her knees, she vomited in the dirt.

If only she could curl up in the grass and take a nap—long enough for the pain to stop.

Alec pressed a wet cloth against her face. He stroked her hair off her forehead and then pressed her head against his shoulder.

Wailing sirens in the distance grew louder until the noise threatened to crack her skull in half. Two uniformed EMTs knelt beside her and started asking her questions. She tried to mumble responses. Minutes later, they lifted her onto a gurney and rolled her into the back of the ambulance. She tried to sit up, tried to get Alec's attention, but the sudden movement stole her breath. She fell back onto the pillow and closed her eyes. Darkness beckoned and offered sweet relief against the pain.

Waiting on word about Sarah was driving Alec nuts. He couldn't erase the look of pain that had contorted her face…pain he'd caused. She was here because of him. He paced from the vending machines to the rose-colored vinyl chairs that formed a horseshoe shape around a glass table covered in dog-eared magazines in the Shelby Lake Memorial emergency department waiting room.

Since her brother and sister-in-law waited in the

exam room with her, he was stuck out here with Daniel
and Toby. After the EMTs had loaded Sarah into the ambulance, he'd had no choice but to bring the boys to the
emergency department with him. With their grandma
still in the hospital and now Sarah injured, someone
needed to keep an eye on them.

No doubt they were as upset and tired of waiting
as Alec.

After getting another glare from the triage nurse, he
dug a handful of change out of his pocket, fed quarters
into the vending machine and punched the water button. He repeated the action two more times, then he
grabbed the bottles and headed to the chairs, handing
one to each of the boys.

"Thanks," they said in unison, taking the bottles.
Toby twisted off the cap and guzzled his water while
leafing through a past issue of *Sports Illustrated.*

Daniel set his bottle in his lap before returning his
focus to the TV, where a game show host called out to
the audience, who responded with cheering and en-
thusiastic applause. He crossed his arms over his chest
and slumped deeper into the chair, purposely turning
away from Alec.

Not that he could blame the kid. Maybe he should
talk to him, but what could he say? He hadn't been the
most compassionate person to them.

Truth be told, he'd been acting like a jerk.

He could still keep his distance but perhaps offer a
little comfort.

Alec sat next to Daniel and sipped his water. At least
it gave him something to do. The magazines held no
appeal, and the TV gave him a headache. Leaning forward, he rested his elbows on his knees and looked at
Daniel. "You okay?"

Jaw tight, Daniel glanced at him, shrugged, then nodded. "Fine." He sat straighter in the chair and looked toward the entrance of the emergency department. "What's taking so long?"

Alec sighed and shook his head. "No idea. If we don't hear anything soon, I'll check in with one of the nurses."

Daniel glared at Alec, then returned his eyes to the obnoxious game show. "We'd never hurt her."

Alec placed a hand on the kid's shoulder, feeling him stiffen. "What happened on the field was an accident. It's my fault she got hurt."

He shook off Alec's hand and jumped to his feet, his fists knotted at his sides. "I'm not talking about that."

"Then what?"

The kid's chest rose and fell rapidly. "I heard what you said on the porch the other day."

Alec pushed to his feet, glanced at the other people in the waiting room watching their heated exchange and nodded to the door. They didn't need an audience. "Let's step outside if you want to talk, so we don't disturb the others."

"Fine." Daniel pushed his way through the chairs and stomped to the exit.

After letting Toby know where he was headed, Alec followed Daniel.

The afternoon heat slammed him in the face. A sheen of sweat slicked his skin. Alec glanced around looking for Daniel and found the kid sitting on a bench facing the Shelby River, which ran parallel to the hospital grounds.

Alec sat next to him and reached for a leaf. Twirling it between his fingers, he asked the question hovering between them. "What did you hear me say?"

"That you don't trust us."

Alec exhaled slowly, then rubbed a thumb and finger over his eyelids. "Listen, man, it's not about you… directly."

"You treat us like we have a disease. I don't know why Sarah asked you to help us cook anyway. You don't like being there. Why not bail if you hate us so much?"

"I don't hate you. Besides, I gave Sarah my word."

"Maybe she should give it back."

Alec laughed.

"You think this is funny?"

"No, kid, I don't."

"I'm not a kid."

"Yes, you are. At least you should be. Listen, Daniel, I'm sorry. Okay? What I said to Sarah had nothing to do with you—I mean that." He repeated the same story about Justin that he'd shared with Sarah at the beginning of the summer. Alec blinked several times, trying to erase the pictures from the past flickering in his head, and rubbed his hands together, suddenly feeling cold. His gut twisted.

Silence floated between them until Daniel cleared his throat. "I'm sorry, man."

"Thanks. Me, too."

"It wasn't your fault."

"So people keep saying. Justin didn't see it that way."

"So I guess I get why you don't like teenagers, but we're not all like that punk, you know?"

"You know, Daniel, my head agrees with you, but…" He paused and pounded on his chest, his throat thickening. "My heart is still struggling with the difference."

"So whatcha gonna do about it? You can't go through life hatin' on teenagers."

"I know. I'm trying."

Before Alec could continue, someone called their

names. They stood and turned to find Toby standing outside the emergency department door, waving them in.

They strode across the grass and parking lot and headed inside to find Caleb Sullivan, Sarah's brother, standing in the waiting room. Alec went over to him and held out a hand. "Hey, man, how's Sarah?"

Caleb shook Alec's hand. "She has a sprained wrist. X-rays showed no broken bones, not even a fracture."

Relief washed over him like a cool shower. The knots in his gut loosened. While annoying, her injuries were treatable. "Well, that's good. What about her head?"

"No concussion, but she has a nice goose egg. She'll probably have a headache and end up with a colorful bruise."

"Wow, I'm surprised. What about the vomiting?"

"Apparently she woke up not feeling well but didn't want to back out of the game. Add in the heat, not drinking enough water and then that sweet homer I heard about—her body'd had enough. Probably heat exhaustion."

Alec's mouth curved into a smile as he remembered how she'd rounded those bases. "Yeah, it was a nice hit. When will she be released?"

"Zoe's helping her get dressed now, so they'll be out shortly."

"Great. I can give her a ride home. Her car's still at the field."

"Actually Zoe mentioned taking her back to our house."

Alec glanced at Daniel and Toby watching their exchange. He stuffed his hands in his pockets and sighed. "Listen, I don't want to get in the middle of a family decision, but if Sarah's at your house, then who will keep the boys?"

Caleb shot them a startled glance. "Oh, man, that's right. Sorry, guys. With all the excitement, I had forgotten you were staying with Sarah for a couple of days. Of course, you can come, too. The house will be packed, but you guys can camp out in our son Griffin's room."

Again, Alec hated to stick his nose where it didn't belong, but Sarah's best interests prodded him to speak up. "Do you think Sarah will get much rest with your little monkeys wanting to hang all over her? From what I hear, Auntie Sarah ranks up there with puppies and Disney princesses."

Caleb laughed and rubbed a hand over his jaw. "Right. I hear what you're saying, but I don't want her to be alone."

"She won't be alone. The boys are pretty responsible, and I'll be downstairs."

Caleb leveled Alec with a direct stare that forced him to break eye connect. He wasn't sure he wanted to know what was going through the man's head. "Dude, you seem awfully interested in my sister."

Alec rolled his eyes. "Don't be ridiculous. I feel bad about what happened to her. That's all."

"If that's the story you're sticking to—"

"Knock it off, Sullivan—" He swallowed the rest of his words as Zoe and Sarah walked into the waiting room. Under the fluorescent lights, her skin was as washed out as the gray floor tiles. Her right arm was wrapped in a supportive bandage. A streak of dirt still marred her face, but it did little to detract from those high cheekbones or those meadow-green eyes.

Alec greeted Zoe with a quick, one-armed hug before turning his attention to Sarah. "How are you feeling?"

"Like I collided with a freight train…or a six-foot catcher."

Alec scowled. "I'm really sorry I hurt you."

"It was an accident. You're not to blame."

"Would you like to go home?"

"Yes, but Zoe mentioned going to their place." Fatigue laced her words.

Alec relayed his conversation with Caleb, and Sarah smiled. "Thanks. I love my nieces, but right now I want to sleep."

Alec placed a hand at the small of her back and guided her to the door. "Let's get out of here, then."

After thanking Caleb and Zoe, they headed for the parking lot. Alec helped Sarah into the passenger seat while the boys piled into the back. He'd get them home so Sarah could relax for the rest of the night. Then he could remind himself she wasn't his problem.

Only he knew he wouldn't sleep well tonight worrying about her.

He pulled out of the parking lot, headed down Center Street, and less than five minutes later he turned into his driveway. Apparently it was long enough for Sarah to fall asleep. Must be the painkillers the doctor had given her.

After parking the car, he opened her door and shook her gently. "Wake up, sleepyhead. We're home."

Her eyelids fluttered as a sweet smile spread across her face. She palmed his cheek. "You're cute."

He grinned. Yep, definitely the painkillers. Wrapping his arm around her shoulder, he guided her out of the car and up the stairs…sort of like helping a baby goat learning to walk.

Once she was settled on her couch, he covered her

with the knitted afghan tossed over the arm. "You sure you'll be okay tonight?"

"Yes, the boys will be here. I'll figure out something for tomorrow."

"What do you mean?"

"The boys are going to the movies with our church youth group. I'm supposed to chaperone, but I'll call Nate to get someone to cover me."

"So you'll be alone?"

"Just in the evening, but I can hang out at my brother's. The girls think I'm kind of fun."

Not just the girls.

Instead of dwelling on that sudden thought and before common sense kicked in, he spoke. "How about if we hang out at my place? I'll cook dinner, and then we can watch *My Fair Lady*."

"Will there be popcorn?"

"As long as you're not making it."

She stuck her tongue out at him. "One little smoke alarm…"

"You're gaining some pretty good cooking skills, but I don't know if you're a popcorn master just yet."

Sarah's eyelids fluttered. "Alec?"

"What?"

"Tell me something." Her voice slurred.

"Anything."

"Was I safe?"

Alec resisted brushing a kiss across her forehead. "Most definitely."

She closed her eyes, a smile curving her mouth. Seconds later, her breathing evened out.

He reached into his wallet and pulled out a business card, handing it to Daniel. "Give me a call if you need anything. I'll bring up some dinner for you guys in a bit."

"Thanks, will do."

Alec closed the door behind him and headed down the steps. Tomorrow's dinner and movie was not a date. Just helping out a friend.

How many times would he have to repeat it for his heart to believe it?

Chapter Nine

Why was Alec so nervous?

He'd been alone with Sarah before. Many times. So what made tonight any different?

Staring at his reflection in the mirror, Alec adjusted the rolled cuffs of his blue-and-white-striped button-down shirt for the third time. He gave his hair a final brush, then left the bathroom, flicking off the light.

The oven timer dinged, setting off a trail of fire-crackers inside his chest. A knot coiled in the pit of his stomach. Maybe this was a mistake.

He fished his phone out of his back pocket, thumbed through his contacts to find Sarah's number and then hovered a moment over her name.

What was he going to do? Call and cancel? For what reason? Because he was a big chicken? Afraid to put himself out there? Or more specifically—his heart?

The doorbell rang. His heart skittered across his ribs. Stowing his phone, he wiped his sweaty palms on the thighs of his jeans and pushed out a slow breath.

He opened the door and smiled, about to greet Sarah, only to find Billy, his brother-in-law, standing on his welcome mat. His baseball hat shaded his face. "What's up, man?"

Billy lifted a hand, then shoved it in his jeans front pocket. "Was in the neighborhood and stopped in to see how you're doing."

Alec glanced over Billy's shoulder, then turned his eyes to his brother-in-law. "Hey, I appreciate the drop-in, but now's not a great time."

"You got a date?" Billy snickered and punched Alec playfully on the shoulder.

"Not…exactly."

Billy stilled, then a smile spread across his face. "But a girl is involved."

"No. I mean, yes, but it's not like that. Sarah's… uh…a friend." Alec fidgeted with his shirt cuffs again.

"Wait a minute." Billy jerked his thumb toward the other apartment. "Sarah as in the cute chick who lives upstairs? The one who set off the smoke alarm with the popcorn?"

"How about I give you a call tomorrow?"

"You didn't answer my question."

"No, I didn't. Good night, man."

Billy gave him a sly look. "Yeah, whatever. Give me a call, dude. And have fun tonight." He waggled his eyebrows, shoved his hands in pockets and ambled off the porch, whistling.

Alec exhaled loudly and started to shut the door when he heard Sarah coming down her stairs. He went over to her door and opened it as her foot touched the last step.

His breath caught in his throat as his chest tightened. Her yellow sundress brushed the tops of her knees, giving her skin a sun-kissed look. A coffee-colored necklace made of wooden beads hung around her neck and a matching slim leather belt cinched her waist. Red sandals—wedges—isn't that what his sister called them?—gave her an additional two inches.

One look at her and Alec realized this was most definitely a date. And for the first time since last night, he was glad he hadn't followed through and canceled.

Clearing his throat, he found his voice. "You look lovely."

"Thanks. I'm probably overdressed." She lifted her wrapped wrist. "This was the easiest thing in my closet to put on."

"How's the arm?"

She shrugged. "Fine, as long as I don't move it. The boys wouldn't let me do anything today."

"Good. We'll have to be careful, then." He offered his elbow and then held the door for her, leading her into his house.

Once she settled on his leather couch, he excused himself and headed for the kitchen. He turned on the faucet, splashed cold water on his face, then dried it with a paper towel.

"Can I do anything?"

He jumped and spun around, surprised to find her behind him in the kitchen. "Nope, got it under control. Want some iced tea?"

"Sure, sounds great. Thanks." She hesitated in the doorway.

"Have a seat on the couch, and I'll bring it in."

Ice snapped and popped as he filled two glasses and carried them into the living room, then set them on the coffee table in front of the couch.

Sarah turned away from his built-in bookcases flanking the fireplace. "Impressive book and DVD collections. Lots of oldies."

"Uncle Emmett, Granddad and I watch movies together every Sunday afternoon. Granddad prefers John Wayne films while Emmett's a huge Clint Eastwood or Sam Elliott fan."

"What about you?"

"I prefer the classics. Most anything with Cary Grant, Gregory Peck or William Holden. And, of course, Audrey Hepburn."

"She's in *My Fair Lady*, right?"

"Yes."

"I'm looking forward to watching it, but you must feed me first." Sarah pressed a hand to her stomach.

"Well, let's eat, then. Dinner's ready. It's been such a nice day that I figured we'd eat on the patio, if that's okay with you?"

"Sure. Sounds good to me."

Alec took her elbow and guided her through the kitchen and out the back door to the small patio, where he set the table for two with red-and-tan-striped placemats. He had considered candles, but that screamed date, which this was not. Something he'd wrestled with the minute he saw Sarah in that dress. Instead, he lit citronella tiki torches to keep the mosquitos away.

Once Sarah was seated, he returned to the kitchen and brought out a square platter that held the main course and a glass bowl filled with mixed greens. He set them on the table, then sat opposite of Sarah. He pulled his napkin out of the wooden ring and spread it across his lap.

Sarah rested her hands on the edge of the glass-topped table. "Mind if I pray?"

"Uh, sure." What else could he say?

Bowing her head, Sarah thanked God for the food and then asked a blessing for Alec.

Would God skip over that request, marking a giant black *X* in the No column? He hadn't done anything worthy of a blessing.

She turned her attention to the food. "What did you make?"

He turned the serving fork toward her. "This is chicken piccata on a bed of angel hair and a tossed salad with an Italian herb dressing. I hope you like it."

"If this tastes half as good as it smells, I'm sure it won't be a problem. You really didn't need to go to all of this trouble." She placed food on her plate, then turned the fork toward him.

"Of course I did. I felt so bad about what happened. If I hadn't tripped over you, then you wouldn't have gotten hurt."

The light dimmed in Sarah's eyes as she set her fork on her plate then put her hands in her lap. She lowered her gaze a moment, then looked at him. "So this is a pity date?"

The quiet tone edged with hurt speared him.

"What? No. This isn't a date." As soon as he spoke, he knew it was the wrong thing to say.

She reached for her glass of tea, her voice as cool as the ice in her beverage. "Glad we cleared that up."

Alec pushed his untouched plate aside and rested his elbows on the table. "Look, Sarah, I didn't mean it like that."

"How did you mean it?" She dropped her voice and shot him a look he couldn't decipher.

Sighing, Alec sat back in his chair and scrubbed a hand over his face. "I felt terrible when you got hurt. With the boys gone for the evening, I didn't want you home alone. I wanted to do something to help you—

friend to friend. Dinner seemed like a good idea. And since you haven't seen that movie yet…"

"Pizza would've been good enough. Or even burgers and fries." She waved a hand over the table. "This meal is something you'd find in a nice restaurant with linen tablecloths, candles and servers who wear black pants and bow ties."

She stood, her chair skidding on the concrete, and placed her napkin next to her untouched plate. Her cheeks matched the red stripes on the placemats. "Thank you for going to all of this trouble, but it wasn't necessary. I'm sorry, but I need to go."

Alec jumped up, his napkin falling to the patio floor. He rounded the table and hurried after her. He pressed a palm against the back door, preventing her from opening it. "Sarah, wait. I'm sorry. I didn't mean to embarrass you. I've made a complete mess of this. This wasn't a pity date. I wanted to make you dinner to help you out. As for the date part…can we not label tonight and just be two friends having dinner? That is, if I can find room around the foot in my mouth?"

She lifted her eyes swimming with vulnerability. "Is that what we are? Friends?"

He raked his fingers through his hair. "I like to think so. The thing is, I don't date."

"Why not?"

"It's complicated." He rubbed his bare ring finger.

Sarah crossed her arms over her chest. "I'm a college-educated woman who works with teenagers on a regular basis. Believe me, I understand complicated."

"Since my wife died, I've had no desire to see anyone else."

"I see."

He tipped up her chin. "It has nothing to do with you—it's me."

"If I had a quarter for every time I heard that, I'd be fifty cents richer. I didn't come here looking for anything beyond dinner and decent company, Alec. Seriously." She laid a hand on his arm. "This can be a nondate, for all I care. I just don't want to be pitied."

A slight breeze ruffled her hair. He brushed a wisp off her cheek and cracked a smile. "I don't pity you, except maybe your popcorn-making skills."

"One time and a girl is marked." She slugged him playfully on the shoulder.

"I'm sorry for lousing up this dinner. Let's start over. Our chicken piccata is getting cold."

Sarah stood at the edge of the patio, her gaze drifting toward the stream cutting through the backyard. Then she turned and glanced at their places at the table. She tossed him a quick grin over her shoulder that nearly buckled his knees. "Let's do something about that."

As she seated herself back at the table and smiled at him again, he realized something—he appreciated the way Sarah challenged him. He was beginning to have her constantly in his thoughts. And that scared him. What would happen if he spent more time with her outside of the community center or his uncle's house? What if he asked her on a real date? Maybe it was time to risk it and find out.

If Sarah could get through the rest of the evening without humiliating herself, then she'd consider that a major accomplishment.

Alec took his seat opposite her, and Sarah forced herself to pick up her fork even though her appetite had disappeared. All she wanted now was to go back upstairs, trade her sundress for pajamas and bury her nose in a romance novel.

Why had she read more into the evening than Alec intended? Of course, he was only trying to help her out. And she appreciated that. She did. But...

Maybe it was the recent playfulness or perhaps the tender way he'd cared for her at the field and then on the way home from the hospital.

Whatever it was—something had shifted in their relationship, but apparently it was one-sided...her side.

"You're not eating. Change your mind?"

Yes.

She smiled and shook her head. She twirled pasta into the bowl of her spoon and put it into her mouth, the lemony flavor immediately bathing her tongue. "Alec, this is really good."

"Glad you like it." His smile created a fluttering like butterfly wings in her stomach.

"What's in this?" She moved one of the small pea-like things with the tines of her fork. Focusing on the meal kept her head where it needed to be instead of venturing into dangerous territory.

"Breaded chicken breasts in a butter and lemon sauce, then I added a sprinkle of capers on top." Alec poked one of the capers with his fork and held it up to show her.

"Capers?"

"They're unripened flower buds that are sun-dried, then pickled."

"I learned something new. You're wasting your talents in real estate. You should have your own restaurant."

"Nah, I don't have the skills needed for that. I've enjoyed cooking since I was about Daniel's age. I don't want to lose my love for it by doing it as a profession."

"I can understand that."

Alec toyed with his pasta, then glanced at her. "May I ask you a question that's none of my business?"

She wiped her mouth with her napkin, then smoothed it back across her lap. "Um, sure, I guess."

"You mentioned you'd have fifty cents over the 'it's not you, but me' thing. Who owes you the first quarter?"

Sarah set her fork on her plate and wiped her mouth on her napkin. "Adam and I dated for four years—since college. Six weeks before our wedding, he called it off, claiming he wasn't ready for a commitment of that magnitude."

"You were together for four years before he decided that?"

"Apparently. But the kicker was he married someone else three months later, and now his new wife is pregnant."

"Man, that stinks."

"Yeah, something like that. I couldn't continue working with him, so I quit my job as youth director at the same church where he led worship and moved to Shelby Lake to help Caleb with the girls. He'd only been here a couple of months and had his hands full."

"I remember. I sold him his house."

"That's right. He and Zoe have talked about moving into something bigger, but for now it meets their needs. Anyway, when they returned from their honeymoon, I needed to find my own place. When your grandma learned I was searching for an apartment, she said she had the perfect place for me. I'm glad you didn't give me the boot after I set off the smoke alarm."

He smiled, causing her insides to flutter again. "Believe me, I was so tempted, but you signed a lease and paid for the summer in advance. I had no legal grounds for eviction. Why only three months?"

"Quite honestly, I'm not sure what I want to do with my life yet. Like I've mentioned before—the outreach program's a trial run funded by a grant. If it's a success, then there's a strong chance the church will keep it going permanently. Right now, we're trying to reach out to kids who may not attend church and build those relationships so they will want to come on a regular basis. We're talking about doing a pilot after-school program. Plus, I've applied to be a mission coordinator with Proclaim Missions. One of my good friends is the director...and he's also Adam's brother. There may be an opening in the fall, but it's kind of a long shot."

"So if the outreach program is a success and you're offered a full-time position and this position opens up with Proclaim Missions, how will you choose?"

"Prayer. Plus, other factors will come into play—my brother and his family are here, I'm getting to know the teens...you know, those kinds of things."

You.

But, of course, she couldn't say that.

"You mentioned your brother and Zoe, but not much about your parents." He leaned back in his chair, focusing his attention on her as if he were genuinely interested in learning more about her.

"My parents live outside of Pittsburgh. My dad is a workaholic. Last year he had a mild heart attack and needed a stent. The day he was released from the cardiac hospital, he went back to his office. He continues to choose work over family. My mom does a lot of volunteer work and sits on various committees." She paused a moment and lifted her face to the evening sun. She chose her next words carefully, not wanting to see another look of pity in Alec's eyes. "I'm sure they love us in their own way, but appearances mean everything to them. Dad wanted Caleb to take over the family business, but he wanted to be a cop. Mom thinks I need to be married and raising babies. I want a husband who makes marriage and family a priority, not an afterthought."

"I can appreciate that. My parents had a great marriage, even with Dad's long deployments and changes in duty stations. When he was home, my favorite memory was watching them after dinner. They'd clean up the kitchen together, always listening to the radio. When a favorite song came on, Dad would take Mom into his arms and dance with her. I think that's what kept her going during those long months when he was away." His voice trailed off as if he had gotten caught up in the memory.

"That's beautiful. How long were they married?"

Alec blinked several times, refocusing on her. "Almost seventeen years. I was fifteen and Chloe was twelve when Dad was killed by friendly fire. We moved to Shelby Lake to live with Gran and Granddad so we could finish school."

"Does your mom still live here?"

"No, she's a nurse and married Bert, a doctor she met at Shelby Lake Memorial. They travel to developing countries to help pregnant women get prenatal care."

"Wow, that's pretty impressive. You've dealt with a lot of loss in your family. How do you do it?"

"Do what?"

Sarah lifted a shoulder. "You know—live. Get out of bed every day."

Alec released a hollow laugh. "If you ask my family, I've only been going through the motions of living since Christy died. Other people are relying on me. I need to be there for them, to help care for them, to keep them safe."

She likened him to a chesty bulldog, teeth bared, watching over his family. "That's a pretty heavy burden to carry."

Alec pushed back his chair and crossed the patio to the lawn. "Every time my dad left for a new deployment, he'd say it was my job to be the man of the house while he was away."

"That's a lot of responsibility to heap on a kid."

"Yeah, well, I'm not a kid anymore. It's up to me to make sure the family stays safe."

"You're the family watchdog, and I admire that about you, Alec. But you can't protect everyone." She stood, walked over to him, pressing a hand to his arm. "Who cares for you?"

His eyes grazed her face, then settled on her hand. "I'm fine."

The way he refused to meet her eyes contradicted his words.

"Are you? Really? Even if your family says you're going through the motions of living?"

"I had it all, Sarah—a nice house, a career, a beautiful wife, a baby on the way. But in one night, I lost everything because of the choices I made." He jerked his hands in the air, pain contorting his face. "By protecting one family, I lost my wife and baby."

"Since you couldn't save your own house, you walked away from your career as a firefighter."

"What choice did I have?" The anguish in his voice knifed her chest. She wanted to wrap her arms around him, but a hug wouldn't erase away his painful past.

A surge of tears warmed her eyes. She hated to see

him hurting, his pain cementing him off from true happiness. "We have to make choices every day. We have to lean into God and trust Him to help us put one foot in front of the other. When life breaks our hearts, trusting God may be all we have."

He scoffed and shook his head. "Easy for you to say. Have you lost someone you loved?"

"When Adam broke our engagement, I was crushed, but when I learned he married someone else three months later, I was devastated. I may not have lost him tragically the way you lost Christy, but my heart was broken. I'm still mourning the aftereffects of that lost relationship…the loss of having my life mapped out. But I know God is with me every step of the way."

"How do you know that?"

"Faith."

"It can't be as simple as that."

"It's as simple as making a choice."

Alec headed back to the table and reached for their empty plates. "I'm going to clear some of these dishes."

Apparently she'd gone too far, and now he was shutting down. "I'll give you a hand."

"No, you sit."

"Don't be silly. I've done enough sitting. Besides, wasn't there a movie option included in this nondate?"

She carried the salad bowl into the kitchen, rummaged through his cupboards to find storage containers and helped stow leftovers in the fridge. With all the time they'd spent in his kitchen during cooking lessons, she moved around the room with a sense of confidence and familiarity, even though it was clearly his domain.

Once the final dish had been loaded into the dishwasher and the machine started, Alec refilled their glasses with tea and carried them into the living room, then set them on the apothecary table. He removed the DVD from the case and inserted it into the player. Settling at the opposite end of the couch, he reached for the remote and pressed Play.

Part of her wanted to scoot closer to him, but she had to remind herself that's not what "just friends" did. After all, this wasn't a date. Instead, she curled up in the other corner of the couch, tucking her feet underneath her, and rested her head on her arms. With a full stomach and a cozy spot, her energy drained out of her and into the couch cushion.

For nearly three hours, they watched the movie in silence with the exception of an occasional laugh and Alec's humming along with the songs.

She struggled to keep her attention on Eliza's plight.

She slid a sideways glance at Alec only to find him watching her. The moment their eyes connected, he returned his gaze to the TV. What was he thinking about? Had her words given him something to ponder? Or would he use them to construct a new barrier between them?

Swallowing a sigh, she forced her attention back to the TV. Once the credits rolled, she stretched and smiled, her eyes drowsy. "That was a great movie. Thanks for insisting I watch it."

"Anytime."

Smiling, she stood and yawned. "It's late. I should go."

"I'll walk you upstairs." He placed a hand at her back.

"Alec, I'm sure I can manage."

"Humor me." After opening his front door, he followed her upstairs to her apartment.

"Thank you for dinner and the movie. Since I was too full for popcorn, I won't hold that against you."

He laughed, the rich sound draping around her like a soft blanket warmed from the dryer. "Next time."

So there was to be a next time?

"You have a nice laugh. You need to use it more often."

His head shot up, and he shot her a quizzical look as if her comment had taken him aback. Sure, he'd laughed before, but it wasn't something he did often. Maybe she could help him change that. Would he even want her to?

"Anyway, I should take some medicine and head to bed." She laid a hand on his arm. "Thanks for everything, Alec."

He leaned forward as she turned her head. His lips brushed hers in the gentlest, barest of kisses. But it was enough to send a shock through her. She jerked back, eyes widening. Had he planned to kiss her?

She'd been kissed before, but this accidental encounter caught her by surprise.

Apparently it'd been a shock to Alec, too, as he turned without a word and jogged down the stairs, slamming the outer door behind him.

Sarah stared at the empty staircase, a realization keeping her rooted in the open doorway. She was falling for Alec Seaver. And that brought her more discomfort than the way he'd left after their kiss.

Chapter Ten

Was Sarah willing to risk falling for someone who didn't share her faith? Someone who was still in love with his late wife?

The question kept her awake late into the night.

Nothing but despair could come of that. And she'd had plenty of unhappiness getting over Adam, thank you very much. She couldn't risk her heart with a man who'd already made it clear he had no intention of surrendering his. So how could something so wrong feel so right?

Not that Alec wanted to encourage anything between them—he'd made it clear he wasn't looking for a relationship.

But then why had he pounded on her door first thing this morning, pulling her out of a delightful dream, and asked her to attend the Celebrate the Lake event that day with him? And why had she jumped so quickly at the opportunity?

Caleb had called first thing, asking if Daniel and Toby wanted to go fishing with him and his ten-year-old son, Griffin. Once she saw them off, she'd crawled into bed, considered her day and allowed herself to re-live last night's accidental kiss like a fifteen-year-old.

As for Alec, he acted like nothing had happened when he knocked on her door this morning to ask her to the event. Maybe that's what he considered it—nothing.

She had to stop thinking about it, focus on the present and enjoy the gorgeous day.

Sunlight glittered across the water, raining diamonds across the rippled surface. The stately pines and majestic oaks fortifying the shores cast shadows across the tops of the white party tents set up on the manicured lawn next to Lakeside Lodge, a Tudor-style building that boasted natural woodwork, floor-to-ceiling windows, sleeping accommodations and a dining room with a menu that rivaled a four-star restaurant's.

A myriad of scents gathered in the light breeze and beckoned guests to go in search of the gourmet selections crafted by culinary artisans using their make-shift kitchens as their studios. Foodies from around the county sampled everything from organic honey to intricate pastries that melted in their mouths.

"Here, try this." Alec held a wrapped piece of something on a toothpick near her mouth.

She pulled her head back and eyed the hors d'oeuvre. "What is it?"

"Trust me." He grinned, the expression transforming his features.

Clamping her lips together, she shook her head. "Uh-uh."

"Oh, come on, Sarah. Live a little." The cajoling tone in his voice made her heart skip.

"Believe me, I lived a lot after you fed me a frog leg claiming it was chicken."

The crinkles around his eyes deepened as he fought

a smile. "You ate it and survived, didn't you? I'm simply trying to expand your culinary palate."

"Sorry, bub, but you broke my trust. Now you have to earn it back."

He winked, giving her the barest of smiles. "How do you propose I do that?"

Was he flirting with her?

"Tell me what's on the toothpick, then buy me some ice cream." She pointed to a vendor scooping homemade gourmet ice cream.

He laughed, a sound Sarah was hearing more and more as their morning continued. "It's a grilled scallop wrapped in prosciutto."

"What's that?"

"It's a type of cured Italian ham."

She eyed the appetizer and wrinkled her nose. "I'm not crazy about seafood."

"It's really good. You'll like it, I promise."

"That's what you said about the frog legs."

He circled it in front of her mouth like a parent trying to cajole a stubborn toddler. "Come on…open up."

She rolled her eyes and exhaled loudly. "Last time. If I don't like this, you're in trouble." She took the toothpick from him and bit into the appetizer. The delicate, almost sweet flavor of the scallop melded with the cured taste of the prosciutto, creating a pleasant combination. Okay, so he was right, but did she really want to see him gloat? "Not bad." She scoured the linen-covered cocktail table, searching for another one.

"Fair enough. Let's get you some ice cream for being so brave."

Tossing her napkin and toothpick into a nearby trash can, they wandered over to a booth with a red-and-white canopy that advertised "N'ice Cream."

A slim man with a reddish beard dressed in a white chef coat greeted them. "Hey, folks. I'm Chef Scott." He nodded toward a tall man with blond hair standing behind their makeshift counter. "This is my brother and business partner, Chef Mitchell."

The other chef smiled at them and handed them a pamphlet. "Ever hear of molecular gastronomy?"

Alec nodded, leafing through their brochure. "I watched a cooking show where they featured different recipes such as transparent ravioli."

Sarah peered over Alec's shoulder. "Sounds like chemistry."

"That's what it is—combining chemistry and cooking. We'll demonstrate, but first, what's your flavor pleasure?" Chef Scott gestured to the chalkboard easel standing next to his table.

Sarah read the variety of flavors from basic vanilla and chocolate to gourmet like green-tea raspberry. She turned to Alec. "So many choices. What are you having?"

He studied the board. "I'm going with German chocolate cake in a hand-rolled waffle cone."

"That was fast."

"It's my favorite cake, so it was an easy choice."

She studied the board and tapped her index finger against her chin. "I can't decide between blueberry cheesecake or salted-caramel hot chocolate."

"Both of those sound pretty amazing."

"Yes. I'll go with the salted caramel, though."

"Great choices. Usually ice cream requires hours to freeze before it can be served." Chef Mitchell rubbed his hands together and grinned. "How about ice cream in under a minute?"

Both chefs gathered the ingredients and added them

to two separate stainless-steel mixer bowls. After explaining how much and what was going into the bowls, they attached them to their coordinating industrial stand mixers and turned them on. While the whipping cream blended with the sugar and other ingredients, both guys donned safety glasses and heavy-duty gloves that covered their hands and forearms.

Chef Scott held up a stainless-steel carafe. "This is where cuisine and chemistry interact to create something your palate has yet to experience."

They poured liquid from the carafes slowly into the rotating bowls. Fog-like vapor billowed over the bowls and frost blanketed the outside.

Less than a minute later, they stopped the mixers and scooped the ice cream into the waffle cones, then handed them to Sarah and Alec.

Sarah bit into hers and groaned. "This is so good. And creamy."

"Exceptionally smooth. A little surprising, I admit."

Chef Scott removed his goggles and gloves. "The liquid nitrogen is minus 320 degrees, so the ice cream freezes with smaller ice crystals, making it creamier than store-bought ice cream. Plus, with fresh ingredients, your ice cream hasn't been stored in the freezer for an extended period of time."

Sarah glanced at Alec, then looked back at the chefs. "We're teaching cooking to teenagers in a summer outreach program. Would you be willing to come and give them a demonstration?"

"I'm sure we could work something out." Chef Mitchell rounded the table and grabbed a couple of business cards out of a small basket hanging on the chalkboard easel and handed one to Alec and one to

Sarah. "Here's our card. Give us a call and we can set something up."

They thanked the chefs, praised the ice cream one more time and wandered away from the food tent toward the lake, cones in hand.

White triangular sails dotted the grayish-blue water. A speedboat pulling a water skier sliced across the rippled surface, creating a small wake. Kayakers paddled closer to shore while kids ran from the sand into the lake. Overhead, puffy cotton-ball clouds ambled across the hazy blue sky. Seagulls scuttled across the sand, scavenging for food.

"Such a beautiful day for the Celebrate the Lake event." Sarah lifted her face to the sunshine.

"Last year it rained the entire weekend. Hopefully this year will make up for last year's low attendance."

She glanced at the full parking lot. "Looks like they're on their way. Thanks for asking me to come along."

"Thanks for coming."

They followed a walking path along the shore while finishing their cones. Occasionally Alec's shoulder brushed hers. Purely accidentally, of course, because when she glanced at him, he continued looking straight ahead, his eyes hidden behind the aviator sunglasses he'd put on.

His white short-sleeved button-down shirt emphasized his muscular forearms. Paired with navy cargo shorts and leather sandals, he fit in perfectly for a day at the lake. When she'd arrived downstairs less than thirty minutes after his knock, he'd complimented her on her outfit—a coral sundress with crocheted bolero sweater and leather sandals. His words had kept her smiling to herself for the rest of the morning.

Sarah swallowed the last bite of her cone and wiped her mouth with her tattered napkin. "That was the best ice cream I've ever had. A little awkward eating it with my left hand, though."

"I'd have to agree."

"Imagine that—we agree on something." She bumped his shoulder playfully.

"I'm sure the kids will enjoy the demonstration." Alec stopped walking and put a hand on her arm. "You okay? Your wrist hurting?"

"No, I'm fine. Why?"

"Didn't you just whimper?"

"What? No."

"I thought I heard a whimper." He removed his sunglasses and hooked them over his shirt pocket. He scanned the low bushes lining the path, then he cocked his head. "There it goes again."

Sarah paused and listened. "I hear it, too. Sounds like it's coming from that thicket of berry bushes. I hope a kid didn't wander off. There are a lot of people here today."

"If it was a kid, they'd be doing a massive search, complete with sweeping the water." Alec walked toward the overgrowth and peered into the bushes. He squatted and stretched out his hand, his voice dropping to a soothing tone. "Hey, boy, what are you doing in there?"

Sarah stooped beside him, placing her injured arm on his back for support, and moved branches aside to find a trembling, matted bundle of fur cowering on a bed of dried leaves. The dog's large brown eyes stared at them with fear and uncertainty. She couldn't stand it and reached out to touch him.

The dog's ears pinned back. He growled low in his throat and bared his teeth.

Alec reached for her hand and pulled it back, but didn't let go. "Be careful. Poor thing feels threatened."

Continuing to talk to the dog in soothing tones, Alec released Sarah's hand and crept closer until he was able to sit on the ground near the animal. He held his hand out for him to sniff, then he gently stroked the dirty, matted fur until the dog stopped baring his teeth and turned its head into Alec's palm.

Grinning at Sarah, Alec scooped up the pup and cradled it against his chest, wrinkling his nose. "Phew. He hasn't had a bath in a while."

Sarah knelt next to them. "Pitiful creature. We can't leave him here. I'll call my sister-in-law. Zoe works at Canine Companions, and they have a shelter for rescued animals."

"I'm sure they have enough already."

"Are you thinking of keeping it? My lease states no pets."

"I'm sure I could sway the landlord."

Sarah looked at him. "Are you serious?"

"Like you said—we can't leave him here."

"No, but Canine Companions will take him in a heartbeat. Leona never turns away animals. Maybe he's lost, and his owners are missing him."

"Or maybe he was abandoned with no one to care for him. This will cut our day short, but would you mind if we leave? We can take him to a groomer, pick up some supplies and then post some flyers until his owner is found."

"I'm totally fine with leaving, but what if his owner doesn't claim him?"

Alec didn't say anything for a moment as he continued to pet the dog, his large hand covering half of its quivering body. "We found him. You have a lot on your plate already, so I don't expect you to care for him."

"What about you? Between running a business, helping me, caring for your family..."

"My schedule is flexible. One of the perks of being the boss. We can't leave him to fend for himself. He's lost and hungry. Now it's up to me to help him to trust, to learn to love again." Alec stared off into the distance.

Was he still referring to the dog?

The more Sarah watched Alec's gentle touch with the dog, the heavier her heart hung in her chest. Why did he have to be so sweet and appealing today? Why couldn't he be a jerk and walk away, leaving the poor animal to continue fighting for survival?

Alec was nothing like the man she'd met her first night in her apartment. He was funny and charming and a complete gentleman who put others' needs before his. Except he'd walked away from his faith. And without that, they could never pursue a relationship.

Sarah needed to make a choice, and although it was the right one, it certainly wasn't easy. She had to put some distance between them. Otherwise, she didn't know if she could recover from another broken heart.

Alec lay on the couch, stroking Eliza's fur. It had been a week and still no one had come forward to claim the little fur ball, despite the flyers plastered all around town. She stirred and looked at Alec with those huge, vulnerable eyes.

What if he and Sarah hadn't been walking along the path? Who knows how long it would've been before the sweet girl would have been rescued.

Nobody deserved to live like that. Surviving instead of thriving.

Something he understood all too well.

By the time they'd gotten the dog to the car, they realized the black-and-tan Yorkshire terrier mix was actually a female. Once she'd been bathed and had her fur and nails trimmed, the pup looked nothing like the ragamuffin they'd rescued.

Had it really been only a week since they'd found her? Seemed longer. At least now she wasn't snapping every time he tried to pet her. Nor did she try to hide. How long should he keep looking for her owner before he called it good enough? He needed to make a vet appointment to get her vaccinated and microchipped. Plus, she needed a dog license, but he didn't want to do that if someone was going to come and claim her.

Did he want to risk getting attached only to lose her? The sweet girl needed to know someone cared for her. Someone was going to protect her and remind her she'd never be alone again.

Did that go for him, too?

For the first time since losing Christy, he was contemplating his future. A month ago, he wouldn't even consider it. Now every time he thought about it, Sarah kept coming to mind. Was it possible he wasn't destined to spend the rest of his life alone? Maybe it was okay for him to move on and find happiness again. Honestly, he didn't want to spend the rest of his life alone.

So where did he go from there? How did he put one foot in front of the other and start thinking about romance again? Maybe he could begin by asking Sarah out on a real date and go from there.

Now he just needed to work up the courage to do it.

A thump sounded on the porch.

Eliza's ears perked up. Her head swiveled toward the

front porch. Then she jumped down, barked and raced across the room.

Alec pushed off the couch and made his way to the front door. He grabbed Eliza's leash and clipped it to her collar, then opened the door to find Sarah on her knees rounding up apples with one hand before they rolled off the edge of the porch.

Eliza pulled on her leash and barked at Sarah.

"Let me help you." Still holding on to the dog's leash, Alec snatched a few and dropped them in one of the grocery bags. Grabbing the handles of the rest of the bags, he jerked his head toward her apartment. "If you get the doors, I'll carry these upstairs for you."

"You don't have to do that. I can get them." Fatigue threaded her words, which she punctuated with a yawn, as she scooped up the pup.

"I want to." Should he be concerned that she didn't seem to meet his gaze? He tipped her chin up. Dark circles shaded her eyes. "You okay?"

She turned her face, but not before he caught the welling of tears. "Yes, just tired. Nancy Obenhaus, the boys' grandma, was admitted into the hospital again last night. She developed a blood clot in her leg. They wanted to visit with her while I ran a few errands. I need to head back there."

"I'm sorry." Alec set the bags by the door and touched her shoulder. "What can I do to help?"

"How do you feel about cloning? Another one of me would be great." She dropped to sit on the top step and tucked Eliza in her lap. "For now, I'll snuggle with this little fur ball."

Sitting next to her, he draped an arm around her shoulders and gave her a gentle squeeze. She sighed and rested her head on his shoulder. "I'm tired, Alec."

"I can hear it in your voice."

"I love those boys, and they're so great, you know, but balancing everything on my plate is a struggle, especially now that Nancy is back in the hospital. With working all day at the community center, spending a couple of hours in the evenings to finish up Emmett's house, visiting Nancy, trying to throw something edible together for dinner and then taking the boys back to their place to hang out for a bit…my day is shot. Then we get up the next morning, and it's wash, rinse, repeat. I don't know how single parents do it."

"They do it because they have to. But you're trying to do too much. Part of that is my fault. Forget about Emmett's place."

"No, the contractor comes in August, and I said I'd have everything done by then. I'm not going back on my word after you've given up a lot to help me with teaching the teens to cook at the center. No way is this going to be a one-sided arrangement. We'll be done in a couple of weeks anyway."

"And in the meantime, you're running yourself ragged. Something needs to give before you're the one in the hospital. The rest of the sorting and organizing can wait."

"Is it selfish to want a hot bath and a nap?" She blew out a long breath.

"Go for it. I can get the boys and take them back to their place or bring them here…whatever they need to do." Anything to bring the spark back to her eyes.

"Thanks, but I'll manage. In a minute. Right now, I need to sit for two more minutes and snuggle this precious puppy." Sarah buried her face in Eliza's fur. "Is she responding to her name yet?"

"Not yet, but she continues to make progress."

"Of course she does. Soon she'll be a real lady."

"You chose a good name for her."

"I figured it was fitting after watching the movie, then seeing how darling she looked when she was cleaned up."

"Seriously, Sarah, what can I do to help? And don't be stubborn by telling me 'nothing.'"

Sarah stood, still holding on to Eliza in one arm, and shielded her eyes from the sun. "I don't even know right now. I need to get back to the hospital, check in with the doctor and then go from there."

"You promise to call me if you need anything?"

"Yes, I promise." She handed the dog back to Alec, then reached down to pick up her grocery bags. "I'll stop by later with an update."

She headed up to her apartment as if putting one foot in front of the other was a chore. He wanted to rush after her, pull her into his arms and let her know everything was going to be okay. But he couldn't make that promise because he knew from experience life threw curveballs. He also knew, however, he could help her catch them.

Right now, she needed to know someone cared and she didn't have to go at it alone.

He headed back into his apartment and released Eliza from her leash. She scampered over to her bed and curled up on the pink cushion.

He pulled out his laptop, an idea forming. While they were at the Celebrate the Lake event, she mentioned loving blueberry cheesecake. In fact, she'd wavered between that and the salted-caramel hot chocolate when it came to the ice cream flavors.

He searched online for a recipe and then typed a grocery list into his phone. He'd make a simple dinner for her and the boys to eat whenever they made it back.

And flowers. Just because. Something to make her smile.

With his plan in place, he crated Eliza—not ready to let her roam freely in the house yet—and then grabbed his keys off the side table before heading out the door.

He didn't even try to convince himself he was only helping a friend. No, he was ready to show Sarah he could take the next step…whatever that was.

Chapter Eleven

Any other time Sarah would've jumped at the incredible opportunity her friend Jonah had just presented her, but at the moment, the job offer weighed her down. One more decision to make.

Mission coordinator for Proclaim Missions. It would be so perfect for her—traveling internationally and coordinating work teams. If she accepted the position, though, it would mean moving closer to Proclaim Missions headquarters in Virginia.

Was she ready to make such a commitment? Leave everything behind again to start fresh?

So much had changed since she'd applied for it a year ago. Her life had been mapped out. Adam had encouraged her to go for it after they'd organized a work team to Swaziland. She and Jonah had continued to stay in touch even after Adam ended their engagement.

He was the one who'd told her about it, but he hadn't expected the opening until the end of the season, which would've given her time to finish the summer outreach program. But the post had just become available, and she wasn't sure if she was ready.

Funny how much her life had changed in the past two months.

Now, entering August, she needed to choose between a full-time dream job that would give her life direction— or her newfound responsibilities.

What about Daniel? Toby? The other teens she'd been mentoring. Not to mention her family. And Alec.

Oh, boy. He was making it so hard to keep her distance, especially when he made amazing cheesecake and had a beautiful basket of wildflowers delivered with a card that read, *Just a little something to make you smile.*

Yes, Jonah's phone call complicated things. She'd told him she needed time to consider the offer, and he'd understood but mentioned he'd need an answer soon.

She'd talk it over with Caleb and Zoe later. Sarah knew they'd help her make the right decision. Now, though, she needed to hustle, or she'd be late for work. As it was, she'd sent the boys ahead and asked them to tell Alec she might be running behind.

With one minute to spare, she walked into the community center.

Instead of the usual chaos, the teens were gathered around the large worktable in the kitchen with their focus intently on Alec. She couldn't hear his words, but the way he gestured with his hands brought a huge smile to her face.

As she approached, she realized he was sharing the story about the liquid nitrogen ice cream. Judging by the teens' expressions and enthusiasm, having Chef Scott and Chef Mitchell come in to demonstrate would be well received. And, seriously, how could they go wrong with N'ice Cream?

Alec caught her gaze and gave her a little wave.

"Okay, guys, time to get to work now that the boss is here."

She tried to ignore the way her heart somersaulted. *Get a grip, girl.*

While the teens tied on their aprons, gathered the ingredients for today's recipes and washed their hands, Alec came over and handed her an apron. "Everything okay? Boys said you had an important call."

She slipped it over her head and nodded. "Yes."

He looked at her with questions in his eyes but refrained from asking.

She didn't elaborate. This wasn't the time or place for a discussion of that depth. Besides, she needed to get her thoughts in order before she could convey them to someone else. She'd set them aside and focus on what she was getting paid to do.

The teens had a final week of cooking before they moved on to the other segments of the program.

It wouldn't be the same without Alec here every day. Even though he could commit only to the two hours they'd agreed upon, his presence gave her motivation to improve her own skills and assist the teens to do better.

But maybe it was for the best, as this would help her to put distance between them.

She couldn't ignore that little piece of her heart that reminded her about the way he'd changed around the teens. Since the day she'd sprained her wrist, he'd been different. More open and much less on the defensive with them.

But then her head butted in and she was reminded that he was still closed off when it came to his faith.

Focus.

She had cooking to teach.

"Listen, guys, this is our last week of cooking.

Next week Josie and Nick Brennan will be coming to teach you about résumé writing and job interviewing in the mornings. Then Chloe Seaver, who happens to be Alec's sister and the owner of Shining Stars Early Learning Center, will be here in the afternoons helping you learn about child care. Plus, James Butler, one of Shelby Lake's paramedics, will be teaching basic first aid and CPR."

Garrett jerked his head to fling his hair out of his eyes and crossed his arms over his chest. "I'd rather cook than learn that boring stuff. At least this is fun."

Sarah laughed. "Sorry, dude, life isn't all fun and games."

"Hey, guys, before we get started, I have something for you." Alec pulled an envelope out of his back pocket and tapped it against his palm. "I, uh, have to be honest and say I wasn't crazy about helping you guys cook when Sarah first asked me. But I'm glad we had the opportunity to work together. You've done a great job." He pulled a stack of cards out of the envelope and handed one to each of the teens. "I know money's tight these days, but you've been learning how to buy decent food on a budget. Maybe this will help."

"Whoa. Is this like for real?" Amber looked at him with widened eyes, a smile brightening her face.

Alec nodded. "One hundred percent legit."

"Awesomesauce." She threw her arms around his neck and hugged him. "Thank you."

Sarah peeked over Daniel's shoulder and nearly choked. Alec had handed out eighteen gift cards worth $100 each at the local grocery store. She shot him a quizzical look.

He leaned against the edge of the sink and shrugged.

She walked over to him. "What an incredibly generous gift, Alec."

"Figured it would help their families."

Sarah wanted to wrap her arms around his neck just as Amber had done and lay her head on his chest, but she couldn't do that in front of the kids. Or ever.

Garrett ambled over to them and extended his hand to Alec. "Hey, man, thanks for the gift card. That was pretty cool."

Alec shook his hand and clapped the kid on the shoulder. "No problem."

"Hey, um, you don't have to say yes, and I totally get it if you don't want to, but the thing is I'll be a senior when school starts." Garrett stuffed his hands in his pockets and kicked the toe of his Converses into the chipped linoleum. A red flush crawled up his neck. "Ma keeps naggin' me to start thinking about my future and all that. So I was wondering, would you guys maybe be willing to write me letters of recommendation I could submit with my application to culinary school?"

Sarah smiled and wrapped an arm around his shoulders. "That's great, G. I'd be honored."

"Really? Awesome." He grinned.

"Me, too, man. You'll make a great chef." Alec held out a fist.

Garrett bumped knuckles, his grin growing wider. "Thanks, dude. Maybe I'll study the molecular gastronomy you told us about."

Sarah's chest ballooned with pride. Even if the board chose not to continue the outreach program, she'd consider Garrett's announcement a measurement of success.

A quick glance at the clock showed they had less than an hour left of Alec's time. Since this week was all about desserts, he'd agreed to help them make a basic cheesecake with their choice of toppings. She had Cindy, the church secretary, put out a plea for spring-form pans in the church bulletin. Of course, now they had more than they needed.

Before Sarah could get them started mixing the cream cheese with the sugar, her phone buzzed in her pocket. She pulled it out and read the number on the screen. Her heart slammed against her rib cage. She shot Alec a sharp look. "Start without me. I need to take this."

She hurried out of the kitchen and answered as she pushed through the side door. She gripped the railing as the caller relayed the news she was so hoping not to hear. She replied to questions through the thickening in her throat. Tears slipped down her cheeks as her chest shuddered. She ended the call and clutched her phone so tightly that if she let go, surely she'd fall apart.

The door opened behind her. She brushed the heel of her hand over her eyes.

"Sarah?" Alec's quiet voice snipped the thin thread seaming her composure.

She whirled around and buried her face into his chest as sobs erupted from her.

His arms slid around her and held her close. He kissed the top of her head and murmured words she couldn't make out.

She struggled to catch her breath and regain her composure, but the doctor's words echoed in her ears, causing fresh tears to cascade down her face.

"Sarah, what's wrong?"

Sarah looked up at Alec, his face blurring in her watery gaze. "That was Dr. Nobles, Nancy's doctor. She passed away about fifteen minutes ago."

"Oh, honey, I'm so sorry. What happened?"

"They're not certain, but they suspect it had something to do with the blood clot in her leg. I have to tell Daniel and Toby." The thought flooded her eyes with fresh tears. "This is going to wreck them."

"Want me to get them for you?"

"Yes, please."

While Alec went back inside, Sarah wiped her eyes with the hem of her fitted T-shirt and struggled to pull herself together.

Alec returned a moment later. Daniel and Toby looked at her with alarm. "What's going on, Sarah?"

"Guys, there's no easy way to say this... Your grandma passed away about twenty minutes ago."

"What? No! That can't be. She was getting better. She was coming home." Toby glared at her as his eyes filled.

"I know, honey. I'm so sorry." She pulled him into her arms, his head brushing her chin. He tightened his grip around her waist.

Daniel ground his jaw, his lips tight as he struggled with the news. "What now, Sarah? What about us? We've got nobody."

Moving Toby to her left side, she grabbed Daniel and pulled him to her and wrapped her arm around his waist. "You've got me. I promise nothing's going to happen to you."

The three of them stood on the concrete steps of the community center, clinging to one another and sobbing as their broken hearts collected on the sidewalk. In an instant, their lives had just changed forever. God only knew where they'd go from here.

* * *

Alec hated funeral homes, but he needed to be there for Sarah, Daniel and Toby.

Rows of chairs lined the side of the viewing room at Lakeside Funeral Home. Pale pink walls, plush rose-colored carpet, music playing softly in the background from a piped-in system, and bookcases filled with stacks of books, landscape photos and artificial flower arrangements tried to give the visitors a welcoming feel as if they were stepping into someone's living room. But the open casket was a reminder of their purpose for being there.

Visitors spoke in hushed tones punctuated by sniffling and muffled sobs. Daniel and Toby stood side by side accepting sympathies from those who came to pay their respects. The guys wore dark suits, polished shoes and coordinating blue patterned ties they probably wouldn't want to wear again—anything to separate them from any reminder of the day. Or at least that was how Alec had felt the day his dad had been laid to rest with full military honors.

When Christy was killed, they'd had a memorial service—a so-called celebration of her life—as they had no body to bury. At that time, Alec hadn't felt like celebrating her life. All he knew was his own existence wouldn't be the same again.

Overwhelming fragrance from the sprays of fresh flowers sitting on pedestals around the room mingled with various perfumes and colognes, giving him a headache and clogging his sinuses.

He needed some fresh air, but he hated to leave in case Sarah or one of the boys needed him. They hadn't asked him to stay, but he knew what it was like having familiar support. He'd caught Sarah's eye on more than one occasion as she'd searched the room and found him. Her tired smile kept him in the room.

He glanced at the grandfather clock in the corner. Ten more minutes. Then visitation would be over. The boys could shed their suits and polite smiles and chill out for a while.

Sarah had been right—they were good kids. He'd judged all of them based on the actions of one broken kid a long time ago.

What if he hadn't reported Justin's bruises? Or if Justin hadn't learned of his mother's actions? Then what? Would the kid have turned out differently? Would Christy still be alive?

The last of the visitors left. Sally, the funeral director, spoke to Sarah, Daniel and Toby in hushed tones. Alec couldn't make out their words, nor did he want to intrude on a private conversation, but he saw her give each of them a hug.

The boys looked at Sarah as if to ask "Now what?"

She put an arm around each of them and drew them close. He saw her blink back tears as she comforted them.

"Let's get out of here and get something to eat," Alec said as he moved over to them and placed his hands on the boys' shoulders. Daniel stiffened and remained stoic.

"I'm not hungry." The boy jerked away from Alec and flopped onto one of the chairs.

Sarah sat next to him and wrapped an arm around him. "You need to eat."

Jumping to his feet, Daniel clenched his fists and glared at Sarah, his voice rising. "Don't tell me what I need. You promised nothing was going to happen to us, but then suddenly we were shipped off to stay with total strangers."

"It was only for one day. Because your grandma didn't have an appointed legal guardian, and I had only her verbal permission to keep you while she was in the hospital. Children and Youth Services had to get involved. I have my emergency certification now, so you can come back with me. Ian and Agnes James are licensed foster parents. Besides, they're good friends and related to my brother through marriage, so they're practically family."

"Well, they're not my family. Toby's the only family I've got."

"You have me. I promise to move mountains to keep you guys permanently."

"Yeah, for how long? I gotta get out of here. I hate this place."

Sarah's shoulders sagged as Daniel stormed from the room. A moment later, the door slammed. Toby glanced at her with fear in his eyes, hesitated a moment, then ran after his brother. "He's been like this since CYS came."

"He's angry and hurting. Give him time to blow off steam." Alec wrapped an arm around her.

Sarah sighed, resting her head on his shoulder. "I know. Thank you for staying. It means a lot."

"No problem. That's what friends are for. Let's go find the boys, then get out of here so you guys can relax." They stood and he placed a hand at the small of her back and guided her out the door held open by the assistant funeral director.

They headed outside onto the wide front porch, where Ian and Agnes stood talking to the boys. Seeing Sarah, Toby walked over to her and wrapped his arms around her waist. Daniel strode off the porch and stood in the driveway, looking a little lost.

When he saw Sarah dab a tear from the corner of her eye with her finger, Alec handed her a handkerchief. "Let me take you guys home."

She wiped her eyes, then balled the cloth in her fist.

Toby released his hold on Sarah and joined his brother in the parking lot.

"I hate this. They've been through so much already. It's so hard on them."

"I know, honey." He'd give almost anything to take away her pain. "Death isn't easy on anyone." He tipped her chin to meet her eyes. "It's heroic of you to take care of these boys, but you also need to make sure you're taking care of yourself, so you don't end up sick. When was the last time you ate? Or slept?"

She shrugged. "I don't have much of an appetite. Between CYS and funeral appointments, eating's become less of a priority."

He pressed a hand to her back and guided her to his car. "Let's grab a pizza on our way to the house."

She laid a hand on his cheek. "Thank you. You're a good friend."

Friend.

Is that all he was to her? Is that all he wanted to be?

A few days ago he'd considered their relationship to be more, but then things changed in a flash. Sarah was talking about keeping the boys permanently. Not that it was a bad thing or anything—they needed someone to love and care for them. But building a relationship with someone who came as a package deal was even more of a challenge.

Question was: How badly did he want to be with Sarah that he would even consider a ready-made family?

Chapter Twelve

Baking his favorite cake was the least Sarah could do to thank Alec for all that he'd done the past couple weeks while she had helped the boys through the difficult days that had followed their grandma's funeral.

A boxed cake mix and canned frosting was more her speed, but she wanted to show Alec his cooking lessons had paid off.

She frosted the rest of the chocolate cake with the coconut pecan frosting, licked the knife, then dropped the empty bowl into the sink of soapy water.

How did other people cook without making such a mess?

Sarah took her time wiping flaked coconut off the counters, washing the measuring cups and round cake pans, and sweeping cake flour and sugar off the floor.

She was going to miss this kitchen when she moved. She and the boys needed a larger place to live—someplace that gave them a little breathing room.

She covered the cake with wax paper and made her way downstairs. Spying her mail in the box outside her door, she grabbed it, only to find it was another letter addressed to Alec but placed in her box. That was the second time. Their mail carrier needed to pay better attention.

Balancing the cake plate on one hand, she rang the doorbell and waited for Alec to answer. When he didn't come, she rang again.

His car was parked in the garage. She'd heard him come home earlier and hadn't noticed him leave again.

Maybe he was in the backyard. She stepped off the porch and followed the sidewalk heading in that direction. He wasn't on his patio. She started to head back to her apartment when she saw him sitting in an Adirondack chair under the cascading weeping willow tree that bowed low over the trickling stream that ran behind the house.

Sarah walked barefoot through the sun-warmed grass. Eliza spotted her and barked, running in circles around Alec's chair. He looked up as she approached and turned the book he had been reading upside down on the arm of his chair. "Hey, what are you doing?"

She thrust the plate at him. "I baked you a cake."

He took it and peeked under the wax paper. A slow smile spread across his face. "A cake? For me? Why?"

"To thank you for everything you've done for us the past couple of weeks. I don't know how we would've made it through without you. This isn't much, but you said German chocolate was your favorite."

"I did? When?"

"When we had the liquid nitrogen ice cream."

"You remembered." He scooped up a dab of frosting and tasted it.

"I remember a lot of things." She winced. Why had she said that? "Anyway, I didn't mean to intrude. I can take the cake back upstairs and bring it down later."

"I have a better idea. Let's have some now. We can eat on the patio."

Alec collected his book and an empty glass. He whistled for Eliza, who had curled up in the grass next to his chair. Together they walked across the lawn to the patio.

Alec nodded toward her upstairs windows. "Where are the boys?"

"Daniel's working at the store, and Toby went fishing with Caleb and Griffin."

"You had time to yourself, and you made me a cake. I'm touched."

"Yeah, well, I'd say wait to thank me. You haven't tasted it yet."

"If the rest tastes as good as the frosting, then I'm in for a treat." Alec set the cake on the tiled patio table, then disappeared through the back door. He returned a few minutes later with plates, forks, a knife and two bottles of water. He set everything on the table then pulled a lighter out of his back pocket and lit the yellow citronella candle in the middle of the table.

He sliced two pieces, put them on plates and slid one to her. "Eat up."

"Thanks." She took her portion, but waited for Alec to try his first.

He took a bite, then smiled. "This is really good cake."

"For real? You're not just saying that?"

"I'm serious. The cake is moist. The frosting is perfect. Not too sweet. I'm really impressed. You did a great job."

His words made her feel like a contestant on a reality cooking show facing a celebrity judge and receiving the top score. She took a bite. Not bad. "I guess this proves I was paying attention during your cooking lessons."

"You've done a great job."

He didn't realize how much his praise meant to her. She ate a few more bites, then set her fork aside and picked up her bottle of water. Instead of uncapping it, she rolled it in her hands. "I need to talk to you about a few things."

"Sure, what's up?"

"If you remember, after Nancy died I became an emergency foster parent for Daniel and Toby."

"Right. Something about not enough foster parents in the area or something like that?" Alec finished the last bite of his cake, wiped his mouth and then leaned back in his chair.

"Yes, they had to stay with Ian and Agnes for one night because of some glitch, but usually Children and Youth Services tries to keep the kids where they feel comfortable. Jeanette, the boys' case worker, said since they were teens, they could choose where to go, and they chose to stay with me."

"I can understand that."

"I'm taking foster parenting classes, but this also means I need to find another place to live that's big enough for all three of us. My lease is up in a couple of weeks anyway."

"Are you looking to rent or to buy? I can show you current listings, if you'd like."

"Well, there's something else." Sarah paused to take a drink of water. "The morning Nancy passed away, my friend Jonah called. He's the director of Proclaim Missions. The mission coordinator position he expected to open in the fall became available sooner. He offered me the job."

Alec's head jerked up. "What does that mean? What did you tell him?"

"I said I needed to think about it. I have a lot of responsibilities here to consider. Plus, it would mean moving to Virginia."

"Virginia." His face remained neutral as if she'd said
she'd be moving across the street. "Would you be able
to do that if you become the boys' foster parent?"

"I don't know. The past couple of weeks have been
crazy with funeral arrangements and then moving the
boys out of Nancy's rented trailer. Today's the first day
I've really had time to think about it. I haven't even
mentioned it to Caleb yet. Our summer outreach program ends in a couple of weeks, and I still don't know
if they're going to extend it into the fall. I need to be
able to provide for the boys."

At her words, he felt his ribs constrict with pressure.
"You have a lot to consider."

She toyed with the remains of her cake. "I know.
My family's here, too. The boys are getting settled in
Shelby Lake, and I'd hate to uproot them with everything they've been through, but Proclaim Missions offers a full-time paycheck with benefits."

"Yes, but wouldn't you have to travel? What will you
do with the boys? Being so far from your family, you'd
have to do everything by yourself. If you really want
this job, then you need to reconsider keeping them."

They weren't going to get into that again, were they?
"I can't turn my back on these boys. They need me."

Alec held up his hands. "I'm not saying you should,
but be sure you're making the right choices for the right
reasons."

"I need to pray about it. I can trust God. He has a
plan and a purpose for all of us." Sarah rested her head
against the back of the chair and closed her eyes.

"If you say so." He wadded his napkin and tossed it onto his empty plate.

She sat up and looked at him. "Of course I do. You don't believe that?"

"I believe it's up to us to take care of ourselves."

"That's selfish thinking."

He frowned. "How do you figure?"

"Trusting God requires a commitment to stay with Him even when times get tough. Life is too difficult to go it alone, Alec. If the circumstances were reversed and your wife had been left without you, would she have given up on God?"

Alec didn't respond. He stood and stared across the yard, his expression stoic. The last thing she wanted to do was push, but she needed to show him hope was his for the taking.

"Tomorrow there's a picnic after church. We've invited everyone from the outreach program. How about coming to the service with us? I'm sure the kids would like to introduce you to their families."

Alec scrubbed a hand over his face and turned to look at her. "Okay, fine."

Even though the words sounded as though they had been dragged from his throat, Sarah's stomach fluttered. Maybe, just maybe, this was the opportunity Alec needed to see God was simply waiting for him to come back.

Why had he told Sarah he'd go to church?

The closer the clock ticked toward ten, the tighter the knot had cinched in Alec's stomach. He hadn't been inside a church since Christy's memorial service. And he hadn't planned on going back. But when Sarah had asked, he'd found himself agreeing.

What was she doing to him?

He sat in the parking lot with his engine idling, trying to decide if he wanted to enter the building or go back on his word and head far away from the place that once used to bring him solace.

Now it served as a reminder that God was selective in answering prayers.

Sarah had asked what he was afraid of. At that time he hadn't had an answer. And he probably still didn't. He just knew he couldn't go in there and smile as if everything was just fine.

But debating about going inside the church wasn't the only thing eating him.

How could Sarah even consider leaving Shelby Lake? What could he do to convince her to stay?

Out of the corner of his eye, he caught a flash of yellow at the same time someone knocked on his window. He turned to find Sarah waving at him.

Sighing, he turned off his engine and exited the sanctuary of his air-conditioned car.

She flung her arms around his neck. "I'm so glad you came."

That made one of them.

Breathing in her fragrance, he tightened his hold for a second, almost as if she were his lifeline.

With her arm tucked in the crook of his elbow, they walked up the wide concrete steps and entered the foyer.

Sunlight streamed through the stained glass windows, sending confetti of colored light across the light oak pews and ruby-colored carpet.

He caught Gran's eye and gave her a tight smile. She missed a note, but recovered quickly, blinking several times. Chloe turned and waved.

Alec hesitated in the aisle—did he sit in Gran's regular pew with her and Chloe, or did he sit with Sarah?

As if realizing his struggle, Sarah slid in behind Chloe. Without another thought, Alec sat beside her and forced himself to stay put…no matter how badly he wanted to run.

For the next hour, he managed to make it through the singing, the greeting and the sermon without bolting out the door. Sitting next to Sarah and feeling the softness of her short-sleeved white sweater brushing against his arm helped to keep him rooted in place.

Even when Pastor Nathan asked, "How do we continue to trust God when life breaks our hearts?" and preached about different men in the Bible who continued to trust God despite their circumstances, Alec stayed.

But now he'd give almost anything to walk away from the picnic that followed. If it hadn't been for some of the teens who looked almost as uncomfortable as he felt, he would've ditched the whole thing.

White canopies shaded picnic tables covered in red-checked tablecloths. Long tables had been set up to hold the variety of potluck dishes prepared by members of the congregation.

Kids ran around the tables with balloons in their hands. The teens threw a red Frisbee to one another. Young moms clustered with their strollers and tended to their babies while their husbands congregated around the grill, holding hamburgers and hotdogs overseen by Pastor Nathan. Older members sat in their lawn chairs and discussed the weather and their array of ailments.

Where did the stuck-in-a-rut widowers hang out?

Taking another swig of his bottled iced tea, he

searched the front lawn for Sarah. Maybe she'd be fine with him leaving.

Her laughter alerted him to her location before he saw her. Following the familiar sound, he found her running barefoot in the grass, chasing Amber's little brothers. She'd shed the sweater she'd worn during the service, exposing lightly tanned shoulders. Her yellow dress nipped in at the waist, then flared to brush the top of her knees. With her tousled hair secured with a matching headband, she looked like a breath of sunshine on the cloudy day.

Spying him, she gave him a little wave. With a hand on her chest, she staggered toward him and leaned on his arm to slide her feet back into her sandals. "Save me. They're wearing me out."

Alec slung an arm around her shoulders. "Showing your age, are you?"

"Yes, I think so."

"Need a drink?" He gestured to his half-empty bottle.

"Yes, please."

They headed to the coolers filled with ice and beverages. Sarah chose water, uncapped it and drank several swallows. She nodded toward the teens hanging out at one of the tables filled with items highlighting what the church had to offer, including several photo albums showcasing different events through the years. "You think they're enjoying themselves?"

He shrugged. "They were throwing a Frisbee a few minutes ago."

"Let's go talk to them."

As they approached the table, Amber glanced at them, then dropped her gaze to the open photo album. She looked at them again and then back to the pictures.

"Hey, Alec? This you? If not, this guy sure looks enough like you to be your twin."

"I don't have a twin." He leaned over her shoulder and looked at the photo she'd marked with her finger— a candid shot of him and Christy at the annual church picnic a year and a half after they were married. He sat with his back against a tree and his arms wrapped around his very pregnant wife. She had turned to say something, and whoever took the picture snapped the photo as he dropped a kiss on the tip of her nose.

The air whooshed out of him as if Amber had jabbed her elbow below his rib cage. He forced a smile. "Yes, that's my late wife, Christy, and me."

"Oh. Sorry." She turned the album page quickly as pink colored her cheeks.

"No need to apologize. She's been gone several years." He gave her shoulder a light squeeze, then drained the last of his iced tea. "Excuse me."

He strode away from the table, pitched the bottle in the trash near the food table and fished his keys out of his pocket as he headed for the parking lot.

"Alec, wait." Sarah jogged alongside him and pressed a hand on his arm. "You okay?"

"Yes."

"Then why are you leaving?"

He scrubbed a hand over his face. "I just… I need to clear my head, okay?"

She stepped up on the parking berm in front of his car. "Call me if you need anything, okay?"

He nodded without speaking, unlocked the car then slid behind the wheel. The caged heat nearly choked him. Cranking the AC, he left the parking lot and headed west on Center Street toward the lake. As the business district grew smaller in his rearview mirror, he passed a familiar road he hadn't traveled in years. He made a sudden U-turn in the middle of the empty street and turned right onto Meadowbrook Drive.

Trees lined either side of the narrow two-lane road. Sunlight flickered through the branches. A squirrel raced across the pavement. Alec swerved to miss it, then slowed his car and turned left, bringing his car to a complete stop.

Gripping the steering wheel with whitened knuckles, he came face-to-face with his past.

He shut off the engine, then opened his door. His feet touched the gravel driveway that had nearly disappeared under the invasion of weeds.

The barren stretch of land shielded by the grove of trees hollowed out his insides. The skeletal remains of the house he once shared with Christy had been bulldozed and hauled away. Gone. Grass filled in the scars from the destructive inferno that had claimed the lives of the ones he loved most. A light wind stirred up the leaves swirling along the path he forged through the forgotten landscape.

As he circled the perimeter where the house used to be, he unlocked the door to a dark corner of his heart and allowed the pressing memories to flood his thoughts. Dropping to his knees, he squeezed his eyes shut against the wetness threatening to escape his eyelids and pounded his fists into his thighs. His chest shuddered. He gulped short swallows of air to control the raggedy edges of his breathing.

Why had he come here? To make sure he didn't forget? To keep Christy's memory alive? What good was a memory when he longed for reality?

Seeing that photo had been a vivid reminder of what he'd lost…and what he longed for again. Though she'd reside forever in his heart, he'd never hold Christy in his arms again. But did that mean he needed to spend the rest of his life alone?

He wasn't sure how long he sat on the ground with his arms wrapped around his knees, remembering his time spent with Christy. They'd dated for a couple of years before getting married. She'd been gone almost as long as they'd been together. They weren't all happy moments, but they'd managed to work through their problems. As he scanned the property boundaries, his eyes stumbled across a swath of color. He frowned and pulled off his sunglasses. Pushing to his feet, he trudged through the grass until he found what had caught his attention.

Hidden behind a hedge of weeds, wildflowers in bursts of yellow, purple and white bloomed in a small clearing next to a little pond. A ray of sunshine spotlighted their beauty. He'd been so focused on the weeds that covered what had been, he'd almost missed the array of color that bloomed near the forgotten pond. A family of ducks quacked at him for disturbing their peace. They flapped their wings and waddled out of the water into the grass.

He inhaled the air that had once been choked with smoke and soot. This time, instead of feeling pain, he felt something different…something a little unfamiliar. Something like…promise.

What else had Pastor Nathan said this morning? God wanted to give them a future and hope?

Was that possible for him?

Sarah's laughter filtered through his head. Her quick smile shone like a beacon on a stormy night.

He walked back to the property line, his steps feeling a little lighter. He stooped and touched the ground. "You'll always be in my heart, Christy."

But he couldn't remain stranded in the past and hide from his future forever. What that future held, he had no idea. Nor did he know where to begin. All he knew was that he had to start living again. And somehow he'd convince Sarah that she needed to be a part of it.

Chapter Thirteen

When was Sarah going to learn to stop expecting more than what others were willing to give?

After Alec had bailed on her at the picnic earlier today, she'd kept her smile in place for the rest of the afternoon, but something inside her had withered.

Alec's wife's tragic death continued to torment him, but seeing his reaction to the photo created a chasm between them she wasn't sure they could ever bridge.

That's why she'd been ignoring his texts and letting his calls go to voice mail. She needed time to clear her head—and the lake seemed to be the perfect place for that.

Carrying her sandals in her left hand, she bent down and scooped up a handful of sand, allowing it to sift through her fingers. She sidestepped the remains of a sand castle, its white tattered napkin flag fluttering in the breeze skimming off the lake. She walked to the end of the dock that separated the fishing from the roped-off swimming area, sat and tucked her sandy feet below the water's surface. Despite the hot summer they've been having, the water temperature remained cool.

On the horizon, the sun balanced on the hilltop,

spilling its tangerine hue across the steely-blue water. Dragonflies hovered over the glassy surface before sky-rocketing over to the shore where the frogs croaked and ducks quacked.

The serenity of the lake should've soothed her, but her thoughts tumbled in her head like choppy waves as questions created a whirlpool of mixed emotions.

"Sarah?" Alec's quiet voice startled her, but she kept her gaze focused on a pontoon boat floating across the lake.

"Sarah?" He called again as his footfalls reverberated to the end where she was sitting.

She turned her head to find him standing about a foot behind her, one hand shielding his eyes from the sun and the other shoved into the pocket of his dress pants, which were stained with grass and dirt at the knees.

What had he been up to?

He walked closer. "I need to talk to you," he said in what was almost a whisper.

The threads of vulnerability in his voice laced around her heart, giving it a gentle tug. "How did you know where I was?"

"Daniel told me when I stopped at your apartment." He toed off his dress shoes and socks and bent to roll up his pant legs. The dock shifted slightly as he settled on the weathered wood beside her and dropped his feet in the water. He sucked in a breath as the cool temperature made contact with his skin.

He brushed a piece of hair off her cheek and tucked it behind her ear, his touch no more than a light caress. "I'm sorry I left so quickly."

"I'm not sure how to respond to that." She needed to move away from him—to gain some distance—but her treacherous heart kept her rooted where she sat.

"You could begin by accepting my apology."

The simplicity of his words unraveled the rope she kept knotted around her mounting hurt and frustration. She whipped off her sunglasses and glared at him. "Does that make everything all better? What about the next time something spooks you? Are you going to run again?"

"I didn't run." He glanced at her, then lowered his eyes to the water.

"You walked away quickly. Amber felt terrible."

"It wasn't her fault."

"Of course it wasn't, but your actions didn't reaffirm that to her. When Adam broke our engagement, my heart was shattered. It took months to put it back together again, piece by piece. I simply can't imagine the pain you endured losing your wife and child so tragically. It changes you, redefines you, calling into question everything you've ever believed. But at some point, you've got to stop running."

He reached for her hands, his thumbs brushing across her skin. "I have stopped. That's what I've come here to tell you. Seeing that picture was an unexpected shock. I can remember that day as if it were yesterday. It was a much happier time in my life. I loved Christy with my whole heart. She was a gift from God and we were going to grow old together. But she was taken from me way too soon. Not only weren't we going to live out our years together, but since she'd been carrying our child, the loss was doubly painful."

"Sometimes life really stinks."

"Yes, it does. After I left the picnic today, I drove out to the property where we lived. The burned shell of the house has been scraped away, thanks to Christy's parents. Dirt was brought in and now grass is growing as if that time in my life with her didn't exist anymore. While I was there, I realized I didn't want to continue living the way I have been."

"What changed?"

"I had forgotten, but behind the house there was a small pond. Wildflowers bloomed along the bank. Even though the house was gone and no one lived there anymore, the flowers continued to grow and thrive. They reminded me of you. You radiate light and joy. You're the kind of person people want to be around because you find the good in others. I want to face my future, but I don't want to do it alone... I want to share it with you."

"Oh, Alec." She should have been thrilled by his words, but instead they created an ache in her chest. "I'm so glad you're ready to move forward, but I don't know if you're truly ready to do it with me."

"Of course I am. I just said so."

"You're clearly still in love with your late wife. I refuse to be with someone who can't commit his whole heart to me."

"Sarah, Christy was my first love. She will always hold a special place right here." He patted his chest. "A part of me will always love her, cherish the memories we made together, but that doesn't mean I can't find love again with someone else."

"What about God?"

"What about Him?"

"Where does He fit into your life?"

He remained quiet for a moment. "Does that make a difference?"

The weight of his words pummeled her core. She blinked back tears. "To me, it makes a world of difference. If you can't commit to Him, then I can't commit to you."

"But—"

"No *buts*. Growing up, my dad put work first. When I found Adam, I was sure he was the one, but then he couldn't follow through with his promises to me, either. I'm at a place in my life where I won't settle. Not anymore. I want a man who is willing to dedicate his life to God and to me. The two are nonnegotiable."

"Tell me you don't feel anything for me, Sarah, and I'll walk away." Alec jumped to his feet and pointed toward the parking lot. "Tell me that, and I'll leave right now."

Sarah stood and wrapped her arms around her waist. "You're not hearing me. What I feel doesn't matter if the other person doesn't share my faith. If I share my life with a man who doesn't share my faith, then I'm headed down the road of heartache once again, and I refuse to do that."

"Fine." He raked his fingers through his hair, then enveloped her hands between his. "I'll come back to church."

"It's more than that. Anyone can go to church." She squeezed his hands, silently pleading with him to have a change of heart. "You've got to learn to trust God. You can't walk away and get mad at Him every time something terrible happens. Otherwise, who will you depend on? Where will you land when life pulls the rug out from under your feet?"

"I've coped on my own."

"But it doesn't have to be like that. God created us for relationships with one another and with Him. He offers peace and comfort. Right now, you're still angry with Him over losing Christy. Until you can resolve your anger and heal those wounds, we can't have a future together."

"Of course I'm angry at God— He robbed me of my family."

"Alec." Sarah dashed away a tear trailing down her face. "I think you're looking for someone to blame for your loss, and you're using God as your scapegoat. It's time to stop picking at your wounds and let them heal. Those scars are a great reminder of how far you've come. Holding on to that anger, though, prevents you from moving forward. That way you don't have to risk your emotions and future pain. It's a sad and selfish way to live."

Releasing his fingers and leaving pieces of her heart at his feet, Sarah picked up her shoes and walked away, leaving Alec sitting on the end of the dock. She knew she was making the right decision, but why did it have to hurt so?

Alec didn't know where to begin. Like Sarah had said, maybe that was what made moving forward so difficult. But he had to try, even if it meant facing his future without Sarah. Her parting words couldn't have been clearer. Problem was, she just didn't get it.

He unlocked the back door to Christy's Closet, unleashing the stale air trapped inside for ages.

Flicking on the lights, he moved into a room that was suspended in time. Wooden floorboards creaked beneath his feet with every step he took. Circular racks of clothes remained untouched after four years. He knew that if he opened the register, he'd still find money in the drawer. A cobweb covered Christy's favorite coffee mug like a doily. Layers of dust coated the counter, covering the paperback she'd been reading.

Why hadn't he let his mother-in-law take over the store after Christy's death like she'd offered?

Fear.

What? No way. What did he have to be afraid of?

Sarah's words from last week on the dock echoed in his head. If he let go, then what did he have to hold on to, to keep his grief alive? Around him everyone else's lives moved forward while his had come to a sudden stop.

But he was trying. He didn't want to be suspended in time like this room. He wanted to pack up the past and find his way back to the present.

The floor creaked behind him. He spun around, his heart thudding in his ears.

Chloe stood at the back entrance of the store, tote bag over her shoulder and a puzzled look stealing across her face.

"What are you doing here?"

She shut the door and stepped into the shop. "I was heading home from work and saw lights, so I came around back to see if your car was here. What are *you* doing here?"

Alec dragged a hand over his face and touched the sleeve of a nearby garment. "I don't know. Trying to move on, I guess."

Chloe dropped her bag on the floor, walked over to him and wrapped her arms around his waist. "That's great…about time, too. Does moving forward include Sarah?"

An ache squeezed his chest. He hadn't seen her in a week. "No."

"Oh, why not?" Chloe's smile disappeared. "I just thought you guys had hit it off pretty well…working together and her getting you to come to church."

He disengaged her arms from around his waist and moved away from her. "It didn't work out."

"I'm sorry."

He shrugged. "It is what it is."

"Are you sure there's no hope?"

"Can we talk about something else, please? I don't want to discuss this anymore."

Chloe planted her hands on her hips and glared at him. "Well, tough. We are going to talk about it. You bottle everything inside and then walk away without dealing with your issues. You've been that way since Dad died."

"It was my job to look after you guys—take care of the family."

"No, it was your job to be a teenager. It was Mom's job to be the parent."

"She fell apart after Dad was killed."

Chloe threw her hands in the air, her voice rising. "Of course she did—he was the love of her life. You know what that's like. But look at her now—she's happily married to Bert and traveling around the world taking care of pregnant women in developing countries."

"Every time Dad deployed, he said it was up to me to look after the family, so I did." Alec jerked a thumb at his chest.

"Dad didn't mean for you to close off your heart and carry everyone else's burdens. You're the best big brother a sister could ask for, but I hate seeing you with this vacant life you're leading."

"Why does everyone keep saying that? I get up, go to work, take care of things at Gran's and with Uncle Emmett. I'm not holed up in my house staring at the walls, drinking away my problems."

"What about your joy? I ran into Billy the other day. He mentioned his threat about handing out your number to all the single women he knows."

"Billy doesn't have much room to talk, considering he dates a lot but hasn't chosen to settle down. And he really needs to mind his own business." Alec sagged against the counter and rubbed a hand down his face. "I really thought Sarah could help restore my joy."

"Are you sure there's no chance of that happening?"

"She said she can't commit to a man who doesn't share her faith."

"Oh."

"Yeah."

"Do you love her?"

Alec's head jerked up. "What?"

"You heard me. Do you love Sarah? I think you do. Remember what Dad always said—love is a choice. Loving God is a choice, too."

"I'm really not in the mood to be taken to church."

"Good, because I'm not eloquent like Pastor Nathan. Life is hard, Alec. Going at it alone makes it harder." She paused and tapped his chest. "Surrendering your heart isn't a sign of weakness but of strength. Once you do that, you'll find your joy. By staying mad at God, you can't blame anyone else for what happened to Christy."

"I'll tell you the same thing I told Sarah—God could've saved Christy, but He didn't. I can't trust Him to protect those I love." Alec strode across the room and stared through the dirty storefront windows into the street.

"So you put on your cape and try to be everyone's hero." Chloe's words struck like bullets in his back.

He scoffed and rolled his eyes. "That's a bit dramatic, don't you think?"

Chloe appeared by his side, her arms folded in front of her. "How's Justin, by the way?"

"What does that have to do with anything?"

"He's the key to this whole thing. How's he doing?"

Alec tossed his hands in the air. "How would I know?"

"He writes to you every week. I've seen the letters."

"I haven't read them."

"Why not?" She shook her head. "See, this is one more thing you're not facing."

"He destroyed my life, Chloe! What am I supposed to do? Forgive him?" Alec turned quickly and ran into one of the racks, causing it to start to tip. He righted it and glared at his sister.

She straightened the hangers and whispered, "Yes."

Alec stiffened his legs to keep from staggering under the weight of her answer. He blinked several times. "Are you crazy?"

"I'm not excusing his actions—he needs to face the consequences, but he was a broken kid who looked up to you."

"He blamed me for destroying his life."

Her eyes filled with tears. "Kind of the same way you're blaming God. If you really want to put the past to rest, read his letters and forgive him. Then you can find real happiness…maybe with Sarah."

He tore his gaze away. Seeing her cry on his behalf shredded his insides. "I need to figure out what to do with this store."

If only he had some of Sarah's organizational skills.

Sniffing, Chloe snapped her fingers and held out her hand. "Give me the keys. I'm taking over. You do for everyone else. Let me do for you. I'll call Christy's mom, and we will take care of everything."

Tired of fighting and so ready to put this day behind him, Alec dug in his pocket, pulled out his keys and twisted the one to the store off his ring. "Thanks."

"It's not a problem. You need to learn to ask for help more often. Now go home and read those letters."

His sister's bossiness was laced with love and genuine concern—he knew that—but her request would mean relinquishing his blame on God and focusing it on the only person who deserved it…himself.

Chapter Fourteen

A week later and Sarah was still moping over a guy she'd known only three months. She so did not want to be that girl, yet a single thought of Alec brought a fresh surge of tears.

Life needed to go on even if she wanted nothing more than to finish the novel she'd been reading while up to her chin in pillows and blankets. At least somebody would be getting her happily-ever-after, even if it were a fictional character.

The rain pounding on the roof made her want to crawl back into bed, even though she had gotten up already to take Daniel to work. Instead of lazing around reading, she needed to do some prep work for tomorrow's dinner at the community center.

To showcase their newfound cooking skills, the teens had decided to host a community dinner fund-raiser. The money they collected would go toward updating the center's kitchen, which hadn't seen a face-lift in a decade.

With Daniel working until noon and Toby still at a friend's sleepover, she had the morning to herself. Instead of wallowing in her self-pity, she decided getting a head start on the dinner prep was a more productive use of her time. It kept her mind from going downstairs and from wondering how Alec was doing.

She missed him. And Eliza.

Too much.

Apparently remaining friends was out of the question because she hadn't seen nor heard from him since last week on the dock. His car was gone when she left for the center in the mornings. When she returned home, his bay in the garage remained empty.

The teens had asked about him, but she'd given them some lame excuse until they'd stopped asking. Amber had mentioned he'd sent her a pretty basket of flowers with a card apologizing for the way he'd walked off and to let her know she'd done nothing wrong.

Sarah appreciated the gesture, but that didn't ease the ache that continued to keep the pieces of her heart scattered.

Someone knocked on her front door.

She flung the blankets aside, swung her legs over the side of the bed and hurried to the living room. Her heart stumbled against her ribs.

Could it be Alec?

Sarah tried to slow her steps to the door. She took a deep breath, let it out slowly, then turned the doorknob.

Smiles creasing their faces, Caleb and Zoe stood on the landing, their hair damp from the rain.

"Hey, guys. What's up? Come in." She stepped back to let them in, trying not to let disappointment line her face. They carried in the scent of rain and happiness.

They exchanged looks and wide smiles. "We have some news and wanted to discuss an idea with you."

"Well, come in, then. Want some coffee?"

"None for me, thanks." Zoe followed her into the

kitchen while Caleb leaned on the breakfast bar that separated the kitchen from the small dining nook.

"You don't want coffee? Are you sick or something?"

"Only in the mornings."

"Mornings? Why only then?" Sarah reached for a mug and set it under the brewing station. Zoe's words connected the dots in her brain. She whirled around. "Oh! You're pregnant!" Sarah threw her arms around her sister-in-law then reached out for Caleb. "Congratulations, you guys. I'm super happy for you."

Their faces blurred as she blinked back wetness. She was happy for them. She was. She turned away to get Caleb's coffee, but a tear strayed down her cheek.

He took the mug from her and set it on the table. "Hey, what's up with the tears?"

"I'm just so happy for you. That's all. You know what a sap I can be."

"You sure?"

"Of course. I cried over Ella and Ava, too, remember?" She wiped her cheek with the back of her hand and pasted a smile on her face. "You mentioned an idea you wanted to share?"

"My sappy sister." Caleb wrapped his arms protectively around Zoe's waist, stirring up feelings of envy within Sarah. "Yes, since we apparently need more room, we're going to see Alec today about buying a new house. We'd have to either put ours on the market or rent it out. So we thought that, since you need a bigger place for you and the boys, we'd ask you about moving into our place."

Sarah reached for another mug, dropped in a tea bag and stuck it under the brewing station. "Wow, really? I appreciate it, guys, but things are still up in the air with my job situation. If the board doesn't offer me a full-time position, I will have to look for something else, even if it means moving away from Shelby Lake." She hadn't told anyone but Alec about the mission-coordinator position.

"We don't need an answer today, and we won't be moving until we find something else anyway. Just wanted to put it out there."

"Thanks, I appreciate it. Hey, where are the kids?"

Zoe gazed longingly at Caleb's coffee, then looked back at Sarah. "Hanging out with my parents. We're picking them up after we swing by Alec's. Why don't you come for dinner tonight?"

"Sure. I'm going to the community center to do some prep for tomorrow, and the teens are getting together to make cookies for the dinner, but the boys and I will come when we're finished." She cupped her mug and pressed her back to the counter.

"If Alec's there, then bring him along, too."

"Yeah, well, I don't think that will be happening." She lowered her eyes to sip her tea, hoping to mask her true feelings. Even the brief mention made her chest ache. "He's not speaking to me these days."

"What happened?" Zoe came over and leaned against the counter next to Sarah.

She appreciated the bonding effort, but it wasn't something she really wanted to talk about in front of her brother. "Let's just say it was a difference of opinion and leave it at that."

"If you want to talk, we're here for you." Caleb drained his cup and then carried it to the sink. He glanced at his watch and then looked at Zoe. "We should get going so we aren't late for our meeting with Alec."

"You're right." Zoe gave Sarah a quick hug and whispered in her ear, "Give me a call if you need some good old-fashioned girl talk."

"Thanks, I appreciate it." She walked them to the door.

After they left, Sarah changed out of her pajamas into a pair of shorts and a T-shirt. She grabbed her purse and umbrella and raced to her car. The rain had lowered the temperature. Maybe she should've grabbed a sweatshirt. But she knew once she started cooking, she'd warm up, so she left it.

Rain pelted her windshield as she slowly drove the few blocks to the community center. Heavy wind forced the trees to sway and bow to its strength. She parked in the back lot. She got out of the car, umbrella in hand, but as soon as she opened it a gust of wind blew it, turning it inside out. She raced for the door, getting soaked in the process.

Once inside, she flipped on the lights and dropped her useless umbrella on the floor. Heading to the kitchen, goose bumps prickled her skin.

Being in there without Alec felt strange. How could she have allowed herself to fall in love with him, knowing he had turned his back on God?

Thunder rolled and rumbled across the valley. Lightning flashed, and the lights flickered. Maybe she wouldn't be doing prep work after all. If the power went out, this wasn't going to be the best place to be. Maybe she should gather their cookie supplies and take them back to her place. She'd call the teens to meet her there. It would be tight, but they'd make it work. If worse came to worse, she was sure Caleb and Zoe would let them use their kitchen. Alec's space would be ideal, but asking him was out of the question.

She went into the storage room where they kept their

goods and flipped on the light. Thunder slammed across the sky, shaking the building. Lights flickered again. She needed to get the ingredients and leave. No sense in sticking around with the storm gaining intensity.

Lightning slashed the sky, turning the dreary gray an eerie silver. A loud crack outside the window caused her to jump and drop the bag of chocolate chips she had just grabbed off the metal industrial shelf.

Heart pounding, she raced to the door and reached for the doorknob as a loud zap buzzed like a transformer blowing. The lights flickered again and then plunged her into near darkness, save for the small window that overlooked the parking lot.

Branches lashed out at the building. A blinding flash sliced through the trees. A deafening crash like two railroad train cars colliding ricocheted off the bricks. The building shook violently. The shelves toppled. Chunks of ceiling pelted her head. The wind howled like a wounded animal.

From somewhere in the building, a blast erupted, shaking the building even more and knocking her to the floor. She scrambled to her feet and raced to open the door, but it wouldn't budge. The fire alarm shrilled. The stench of smoke crept through the fragmented wall.

A terror she'd never felt before sluiced through her veins, turning her blood to ice. Her heart jammed in her throat, choking her. With a small square window she wouldn't fit through and her only exit blocked, she was trapped.

This couldn't be happening!

Sarah searched frantically for something, anything to break the single paned window. Even if she couldn't crawl through it, she could cry for help and pray someone heard her.

Her breathing came in shallow gasps. Tears flooded her eyes. "God, I could really use a way out of here."

She really didn't want to die today.

"So do you have an idea of where you'd like to live or what you're looking for in your new home?" Alec crossed to the mini fridge and removed three bottles of water. After handing one to Caleb and one to Zoe, he took his and sat in his black leather chair behind the L-shaped executive desk that had once been Granddad's before Alec took over. He opened his laptop to make some notes. Despite the turmoil in his life, talking houses was well within his comfort zone.

Caleb leaned back in one of the blue padded chairs on the other side of the desk and rested his hand on Zoe's knee. "Four bedrooms and a large backyard, preferably fenced, a couple of bathrooms, garage. Other than that, we're pretty flexible."

Trying not to let the couple's happiness dampen his attitude, Alec typed notes into the form he used to help compile a client's needs. "What about your current house? Planning to sell? Rent it out?"

"We know Sarah's lease is up at the end of the month, and she needs a bigger place for her and the boys, so we offered her the place to rent. I know closing on a new place that quickly is practically impossible, but we figured we'd see what's currently on the market."

Alec looked up from his computer. "If you're rushing for Sarah's sake, don't worry. She can stay as long as necessary."

"Thanks. That's kind of you, considering—" Zoe nudged Caleb in the ribs, interrupting his words. He scowled at her, rubbing his side. "What's that for?"

Alec could see Zoe was trying to send her husband

a silent message with her eyes, but he was either clueless or ignoring her.

"What's going on?" Alec rounded his desk and leaned against the edge.

Zoe smiled and shook her head. "Nothing. Sometimes my husband forgets to mind his own business."

Alec crossed his arms over his chest. "Is Sarah okay?"

"Maybe you should talk to her and find out."

"Caleb." Zoe gave him a pointed look.

Her husband looked back at her, eyebrow raised. "Zoe."

"Guys, is there something I should know about?"

"She said you're not speaking to her right now." Caleb leveled him with a direct, almost challenging look.

"I was giving her the space she requested." Alec pushed away from his desk. A glance out the window showed the storm still battering the streets. The fire whistle went off. Inevitable with a storm like this one.

Caleb's phone rang. "Excuse me." He fished it out of his pocket, glanced at the screen and frowned. "Sullivan."

He remained silent a moment, then jumped to his feet, knocking his unopened bottle of water to the floor. "When?" Deep lines etched his forehead and bracketed his mouth. "Thanks. On my way."

He ended the call and scrubbed a hand over his face as he headed for the door. "Dispatch received a call— a tree fell on the community center, and the fire alarm went off, alerting the department. Sarah's car is in the parking lot."

Zoe grabbed her purse and hurried after Caleb.

Alec's heart stumbled against his ribs.

No, not again.

He raced out the back door to his car. Rain stung his face, but it was nothing compared to the sudden frost that chilled him from the inside out.

He followed Caleb, then jerked to a stop behind the man's car half a block from the community center. Shelby Lake Fire Department's rescue truck and engine was parked in the street, their red lights reflecting off the wet pavement. Police cruisers and an ambulance blocked traffic.

Uniformed officers wearing yellow reflective vests and carrying portable radios held back the growing crowd of curious people huddled under umbrellas. Even the pouring rain didn't deter people's curiosity.

Alec scanned the crew dressed in turnout gear with air tanks strapped to their backs until he found Billy, the battalion chief on duty. He pushed through the growing crowd of onlookers, but a police officer stepped in front of him, blocking Billy from his sight. He lifted a hand. "Sir, you need to stay back."

"I need to see Billy. Find out what's going on."

"They have everything under control. Let them do their jobs." The officer's tone offered no negotiation.

Caleb strode up to the officer and grabbed Alec's arm. "It's okay, Jennings. He's with me. My sister's in that building. Let us through."

Without waiting for a response, Caleb shouldered around the officer and hurried over to the cluster of firefighters with Alec on his heels.

Alec found Billy and grabbed his brother-in-law's arm. "What's the status? Did you find Sarah?"

"Alec, you have no business being here. Get back with the rest of the crowd." Billy jerked a thumb toward the sidewalk and stalked away.

Alec jogged over to the crew and gripped Billy's shoulder. "Sarah is my business. Have you located her?"

"Get out of the way, Alec." Billy turned away as his radio squawked. He keyed the mic and relayed a command.

Heat seared Alec's face as the reddish-orange flames licked the bricks, prowling and stalking like a hungry lion in search of prey.

Hose lines snaked through puddles forming in the wet grass as crews entered the building to battle the blaze from within. A firefighter climbed a ladder and started busting a window with a Halligan bar, a heavy metal tool used to gain entry into a building. The whining of saws and shattering of glass spun Alec's mind back to four years ago when he fought to save his own house with Christy trapped inside.

He couldn't let history repeat itself. He had to save Sarah.

"What can I do to help?" Smoke burned his eyes and choked his throat. The rain offered little relief.

Billy gripped his shoulders. "Stay out of the way. Trust us to do our jobs. Don't be a hero. We'll get Sarah out."

Shouts erupted as the structure shifted, sending showers of sparks into the singed branches of a tree and the fire crews running from the building.

"What's happening? What's going on?" Alec's shouted questions went unanswered.

A cry sounded from the side of the building. Radios cracked and commands were given. Several firefighters hurried to that end where the tree had crashed through the roof.

He tried to make out what they were saying, but the

wind, pounding rain and all the other noises drowned out their words.

Alec wanted to throw on turnout gear, strap on an air tank and follow them into the building. At least he'd have a clue of what was going on. Standing on the sidelines was killing him.

A moment later one of the firefighters emerged carrying something in his arms.

No…some*one*. Sarah.

Thank God.

The crew member hurried across the wet grass toward the ambulance, where paramedics waited. Sarah's arms were wrapped around the guy's neck as she coughed into his shoulder.

Alec's heart ratcheted as his breathing shuddered in his chest.

She was alive.

One of the paramedics—Alec recognized him as James Butler, who had tended to her at the field when she'd sprained her wrist—placed an oxygen mask over Sarah's face.

Caleb hurried over to the ambulance. Hands on his hips, he nodded, and without saying a word leaned over the gurney to give Sarah a hug. He climbed into the ambulance with the paramedic. The EMT closed the door, then raced around to the driver's side. Alec wanted to rush over to them and demand to see her, but truth be told he had no right. He wasn't family.

Less than a minute later, the ambulance lights came on and the siren sounded as it maneuvered past the engines and cruisers to rush to the hospital.

Billy strode over to him, clapping his hand on his shoulder. "Your girl's free. I figured you'd be pushing people down to get to her."

"She's not my girl. I'm not the kind of man she needs in her life."

"What's that supposed to mean?"

"I will only let her down. Like I did Christy."

"Buddy, you did not fail my sister. You did everything you could to save her, but God had other plans. It's time you stop playing the martyr and accept that God has you here for a reason."

"And what would that be?"

"I don't know. But maybe it's time you talked to Him again and found out."

Chapter Fifteen

Alec couldn't stop shaking.

After leaving the scene, he yearned to go to the hospital and check on Sarah.

No, he longed to race to the hospital, scoop her up in his arms and cradle her against his chest.

She was alive.

Thank God.

What? No. No thanks to God.

Thanks to the fire crew.

Where was God when that tree fell on the center?

Where was God when the fire started?

Where was God when Sarah struggled for her life?

Same place He was when Christy was trapped, screaming for help…absent, vacant, distant, nowhere to be seen.

Alec unlocked his front door and tossed his keys in the small dish on the narrow table in his tiny foyer. Inside his air-conditioned living room, the stench of the fire stung his nose even more. He needed to shed his clothes and stand under the shower for about an hour to scrub the smell from his hair and skin.

Instead, he dropped into his chair, closed his burning eyes and sighed. The silence of his house should have been soothing after the cacophony of activity at the scene. Instead of bringing peace, it reminded him of the loneliness that had taken up residence in his chest cavity.

Turning his head to the side, his gaze settled on the pile of envelopes sitting on his desk. Letters from Justin, dating from his first week in the juvenile detention center to the most recent one he'd received a few days ago.

A few days ago he'd pulled them out of his bottom desk drawer after Chloe suggested he read them. Yet he couldn't bring himself to break the seal on a single envelope.

What was he afraid of finding?

Was holding on to that anger so important? Or was he afraid that if he released it, he'd find himself foundering like a drowning victim?

As he closed his eyes to blot out the thought, he imagined an outstretched hand reaching out to him.

His eyes snapped open. He scrubbed a hand over his face and leaned forward, resting his elbows on his knees. Even though he'd removed his wedding ring a couple of years ago, his left hand still appeared naked, as if something was missing.

Not something. Someone.

Sarah.

He missed her too much to put it into words. He missed her quick laugh. Her fragrance. The way she fit nicely in his arms.

Tired of running, he pushed himself out of the chair and marched to the desk. Grabbing the first envelope, he ripped it open and scanned the contents. He reached for another and did the same.

Envelopes fell to the floor. He tossed each letter aside

and grabbed a new one. At some point he settled in his desk chair and turned on his banker's lamp when darkness cloaked the room.

Hours later, fatigue blurred his vision, jumbling the letters on the pages together. Rubbing a thumb and forefinger over his eyes, he reached for the last letter—the one he'd received only a few days ago.

Sliding a letter opener under the crease, he sliced it open and pulled out a single sheet of paper. He opened it up to find two words written at the top of the page: *Forgive me.*

Forgive him?

Was he crazy?

How could Justin expect Alec to forgive him for what he'd done? His destructive choices had robbed Alec of everything he held dear. How was that forgivable?

Alec wadded the letter into a tight ball and whipped it across the room. It hit the wall, then bounced onto the side table, sweeping a piece of paper onto the floor. Alec stomped over to it and snatched the paper, finding it to be the bulletin from the day he'd gone to church with Sarah. He thought he'd thrown it away.

He started to crumple it like he'd done the letter and toss it in the trash when the script on the front caught his attention. It was a quote by Christian writer C. S. Lewis that read, "To be a Christian means to forgive the inexcusable because God has forgiven the inexcusable in you."

Surely nothing Alec had ever done equated to murder.

But he'd gone to church long enough to know God didn't recognize different degrees of sin.

Alec gripped that bulletin in his hand and then picked up the crumpled letter. He unfolded it, smoothing out the creases and read the two words again... *Forgive me.*

With his back pressed to the wall, Alec slid down until he sat on the floor. Images flickered through his head…meeting Christy, proposing, getting married, learning they were having a baby and then the fire. But instead of seeing Christy's face in the flames and hearing her screams, he saw Sarah's.

And he couldn't save her.

What had Billy said earlier? Stop trying to be everyone's hero. It wasn't his job to save Sarah. It was his job to trust God to save her. How could he do that when God had let him down?

But had He really?

Had God really been there in the midst of the fire?

Sure the fire crew put out the fire. But what about the rain? Billy had said the rain had helped to contain the fire and keep it from spreading faster.

But…

A weariness he hadn't felt in a long time soaked through every pore. He was tired. So very tired. Tired of fighting. Tired of being afraid. Tired of being alone.

Pressure gripped his chest. He squeezed his eyes shut against the stinging tears. He buried his face in his arms and wept.

God, please forgive me for trying to do everything by myself. I don't want to be a hero, but I don't want to let others down, either. Help me to keep my trust in You. Help me to learn to forgive and to have compassion. Help me to put the past to rest. Please help me not to be too late for Sarah.

The hatred he kept buried in his heart trickled out, withering the root of bitterness he'd allowed to grow. A peace he hadn't felt in years swelled in his chest.

With no regard for the time, Alec grabbed his keys

and rushed to his car. Ten minutes later, he rang the doorbell and waited and prayed it wasn't too late.

Nathan Kendall, pastor of the Shelby Lake Community Church, opened the door, rubbing his eyes. "Alec, this is a surprise."

Seeing Nathan's T-shirt and pajama pants and noticing the darkness for the first time, Alec sighed. "I'm sorry. I didn't realize it was so late. I, uh, needed to talk to you. It's kind of important. A matter of life and death."

"Whose?"

"Mine…in a manner of speaking."

"Yes, of course." He stepped aside and waved for Alec to enter. "Come in. Let's talk."

Alec stepped inside, ready to take back his life and share his idea for how he could win Sarah's heart. Now he prayed it would all come together.

All Sarah wanted was to be discharged from the hospital and have a long soak in a tub full of bubbles to rid of the lingering scent of smoke. That and a tall glass of ice water. And then to crawl into her bed with a soft pillow. If only she could escape the nightmare that showed up every time she closed her eyes.

The cracking and crash of the tree on the center. The incredible fear that had constricted her. Hearing her own screams being drowned out by the rain and the wind. The pain in her chest from lack of oxygen and the heat of the fire penetrating through her only walls of safety in the storage closet.

She didn't want to live in fear of storms or trees or fire, but every time she closed her eyes, she had to claw her way to consciousness. Sleep didn't bring her relief.

The stench of smoke singed her nostrils. Her lungs

burned every time she coughed, bringing tears to her irritated eyes.

A knock sounded on her open door, which was hidden by the privacy curtain.

"Come in." Her voice still sounded hoarse.

Melissa peeked around the side of the curtain. "Hey, you."

Sarah shifted, raising herself to an upright position. "Hey, you're supposed to be in bed."

Melissa waved away Sarah's concern. "I'm past the panic stage. My doctor gave me the all clear to be out of bed, but I won't be hauling furniture or doing anything like that."

"I'm so glad you're not at risk anymore. How are you feeling?"

"Forget about me. How are you?" Without waiting for a response, her friend sat on the end of her bed and briefly squeezed her arm, and pressed her fingers to the corners of her eyes as tears filled them. "On the way over, I told myself I wasn't going to cry. When Nate called to say what had happened, I hit my knees so fast to pray. I was so scared."

Sarah drew in a shuddering breath. "Not my favorite moment. The center is destroyed." A tear leaked out the side of her eye and slid down to her ear. "Those kids worked so hard this summer. The program has been amazing. That dinner was going to be the final thing to convince the church board that we need to keep this as a year-round outreach opportunity. They're so amazing, Mel. And now everything's ruined."

Melissa looked away and adjusted Sarah's blankets, smoothing out wrinkles. "It's very admirable of you to put the kids first. Right now, you need to focus on getting out of here. When will you be released?"

Something about her friend's lack of eye contact and sudden busyness had Sarah's nerves thrumming. "Melissa?"

"Hmm?"

"What aren't you telling me?"

She smiled. Too brightly. "Hey, how about if I take you home so you can get some rest. You and I both know no one rests in a hospital."

"Melissa."

The woman's hands stilled. She sighed and stood. Moving closer to the head of Sarah's bed, she gripped the bed frame. "Nate should be the one talking to you about this. He's not going to like me treading on church business."

Sarah forced herself to swallow past the lump in her throat. Even though she knew what Melissa was going to say, she pushed the words out of her mouth. "Wha... what should he, uh, be talking to me a-about?"

Melissa tilted her head, her eyes glazed with tears. "The church isn't going to continue the outreach program. They love what you've done this summer, but the grant money is nearly gone, and there are no additional funds in the budget."

"But we can do fund-raisers, ask for company sponsors, apply for new grants." Sarah hated the desperation creeping into her voice, but they had to do something—those kids needed the program to continue...she needed it to continue. Without it, what would happen to them? To her?

"That's something you'll have to take up with Nate and the board. If I can help in any way, I will. You know that. Keep the faith, girl. God's got a plan."

"Yeah." Sarah sniffed and forced a smile. A pounding pulsed at her temples.

Melissa handed her a tissue. "So when are you going to be released?"

"Caleb and Zoe are coming in a little while. They kept the boys overnight, which was something else they had to deal with yesterday. Those poor kids have been through the wringer."

"My offer to take you home still stands. And that way your brother and sister-in-law don't have to round up their brood. We can swing by their place and pick up the boys."

"Are you sure?"

"Yes, of course. Unless there's someone else you'd rather have take you home." Melissa's not-so-subtle comment doused Sarah's heart like a firefighter's hose.

Eyes fixed on her rumpled blankets, she sniffed and shook her head. "There's no one."

"Hey, what's wrong?"

"Nothing." Sarah attempted to straighten her frown into a smile, but it became too much work. Flinging the blankets aside, she moved her legs over the edge of the bed, then stalled as a wave of dizziness washed over her. When she felt steadier, she looked around for her clothes.

Then she remembered. "I don't have anything to wear. Zoe took my clothes home last night to wash… or burn. I'll have to call her to bring me something to wear."

"Or not. When Nate said they were keeping you overnight for observation, I grabbed a T-shirt and a pair of shorts for you to wear home. We were close to the same size before I got pregnant, so they should fit." Melissa moved behind the privacy curtain, reached for a small tote bag and handed it to Sarah.

Sarah pulled out a pink fitted T-shirt, tan shorts and

a pair of pink flip-flops. "You're the best. You think of everything. My shoes must have come off when they got me out of that building."

"I'll step outside to let you get dressed. Then how about if you have dinner with Nate and me? Little Nate would love to see you."

"Thanks, but Caleb insisted I eat with them tonight."

Sarah started to stand then stopped as another thought occurred to her. "My car. I didn't even think about my car. I parked it behind the community center. I'll have to ask Caleb to see if it has suffered any storm damage."

"I know you have a lot to process right now, Sarah, but remember all of that stuff is replaceable. You're not. I'm just so happy you're safe." Melissa slid off the bed. "I'll go let the nurses know you're ready to be discharged."

Sarah dropped back against her pillow as questions pummeled her brain. Melissa was right—she had to be thankful for being alive. And she was. But she had a lot to sort out—where was she going to live, where was she going to work and if her car was inoperable, how was she going to get there?

One thing at a time. She needed to get the boys from her brother's place and then go home.

Her purse...with her phone and her house keys had been at the center.

The weight of all the little things she had to figure out sagged her shoulders to the point where she wanted to lie back on the bed, pull up the sheet and close her eyes. The only way she could get into the house was to ask the landlord to let her in. In other words she had to see Alec.

And his actions lately made it clear he wanted nothing to do with her.

Did he even care that she'd been trapped inside that building?

She'd truly believed they were friends. Above everything else, his silence scraped her heart raw.

Her friend peeked her head around the curtain a few minutes later. "All ready? You're not even dressed yet. Wrong size?"

"No, the size is fine. Sorry. An unexpected pity party."

"Aww, I didn't even get an invite. What was the occasion?"

"I don't have a phone or a house key."

"Oh, honey, forget those things. You're coming back to my place. You can shower and take a nap in the guest room. I'll have Nathan get in touch with your brother about the boys and with Alec to get a key for you."

Too tired to argue, Sarah nodded. Melissa was right—they could sort out the other things later. Too bad picking up the broken pieces of her life would take a lot more time.

Chapter Sixteen

This plan had to work in order to win Sarah's heart… and convince her to stay in Shelby Lake.

After spending a couple of hours with Pastor Nate, receiving counseling about forgiveness and then re-committing his life to God, Alec had gone home. But he couldn't sleep. Energy and a peace he hadn't felt in years consumed him. He'd formed a plan, then first thing this morning, he'd called on his family to help him work it out.

Now he had to prove to Sarah he was the right man for her. That he was someone who had turned the page on his previous life and was ready to start a new chapter with her and the boys, if she'd let him—if they'd let him. He had to gain the boys' trust, too.

He stood in the middle of the former Christy's Closet.

Alec appreciated his sister's willingness to take over cleaning out the store. Paint fumes mingled with the scents of citrus cleaner and the lemon oil used to restore the wooden floor to a polished gleam. The floor creaked beneath the soles of his leather flip-flops and echoed off the bare walls. Not only had Chloe and Jane Lynn, Christy's mother, cleaned out the racks of clothes and accessories, but they'd scrubbed every inch of the place and repainted the walls a buttery yellow that, of course, reminded him of Sarah.

The building with its second-floor apartments offered so many possibilities. Alec could do anything he wanted with it. After talking with Pastor Nate, he knew what that was, but everything depended on Sarah.

The front door opened and, with the exception of Daniel and Toby, the teens from the summer outreach program filed in. Their eyes were wary as they took in the empty room. At that moment Alec realized that if he wanted their help, then he needed to be transparent and expose his flaws. How else would they see him as the real deal?

His gut tightened. This was his first time around them without Sarah. He raised a hand in greeting, then gestured to the stacks of gray metal folding chairs he'd borrowed from the church with Nate's permission. "Hey, guys. Glad you could make it. Grab a chair and let's talk."

Metal clanged against metal as the kids grabbed chairs and arranged them in a circle. Once they were seated, Alec reached for one of his own, turned it around and straddled it. He ran a hand down his face, suddenly tired for the first time in hours.

Garrett, with a serious look on his face for once, folded his arms over his chest and spoke up. "How's Sarah?"

Alec rubbed his hands together, then rested them on his knees. He took in their somber faces. "I hear she's doing better and coming home today. And that's part of what I want to talk to you about."

"You hear? You haven't seen her?" The accusatory tone in Garrett's voice scored a direct hit.

He kept eye contact with the kid. "No."

Garrett ground his jaw. He shook his head, then exhaled. "So you ditched her the way you ditched us."

"Guys, I screwed up. Big-time. And now I owe you an apology and need to ask for your forgiveness. When Sarah approached me with this cooking idea of hers, I couldn't say no fast enough." For the next half hour he shared his story about meeting Justin, Justin's revenge, losing Christy and the way he turned his back on God. "The last thing I wanted was to get involved with a bunch of teenagers again." Instead of the ache that usually pinged his heart, Alec felt more at ease than he had in a long time.

Amber's eyes shifted to her friends, then looked at him. "So what changed?"

Alec stood and shoved his hands in his back pockets. He ambled around the circle, making sure to make eye contact with each of them. "I saw the way you guys really embraced the skills Sarah wanted you to learn."

"Sarah—she's chill, man. She gets us." Garrett fist-bumped his neighbor.

"Yes, she does."

Amber slouched in her chair and shrugged. "So why are you like telling us this?"

Alec stood with his back to the group and stared out the front window a moment. Sunshine streamed through the sparkling clean storefront windows, removing any trace in the sky of the storm that had wrecked havoc the previous day. Branches littered the sidewalks and streets. He turned back to the teenagers. "Because I think it's important to know where someone comes from so you can understand where they're trying to go. Plus, I messed things up with Sarah, and I'm asking you guys to help me fix that."

Amber and Garrett exchanged looks, then Garrett jutted out his chin and gave him a quick nod. "What do you have in mind?"

"Would you still like to have the community dinner to show off your cooking skills?"

"That's going to be tough without a kitchen and stuff." Amber tossed her braid over her shoulder and raised an eyebrow.

Alec turned his chair back around, sat and balanced his elbows on his knees. "We have access to one. Josie Brennan offered us the Cuppa Josie's kitchen. It's not large enough for all of us at once, but we can work in shifts. My family will be here helping set up tables and turning this place into a makeshift dining room. Since Josie's is just down the block, we can make the food there and keep it warm here with buffet-style chafing dishes. Are you up for it?"

The gang glanced at one another, then nodded. "Yes, let's do this." Cheers and slapping of palms filled the air.

Alec pulled out his iPhone from his back pocket and opened the Notes app. "We need to figure out a menu, then go shopping. We need to break up into teams. Garrett, I'm putting you in charge of the cooking group. Amber, can you handle the setup crew?"

When the teen nodded her head, Alec continued. "Great. I'll lead the communications crew and let people know a dinner is happening tonight."

They separated into their teams and went to work. Alec called Gran and Chloe for help in spreading the word.

The front door opened, and Billy entered. Striding over to Alec, he clapped him on the shoulder. "How's it going, man?"

Alec grasped Billy's hand and gave him a one-armed hug. "What's up, Billy?"

"I talked to Ma. She told me what she and your sister did. I'm proud of you, man. I'm sure it wasn't easy."

"But it was necessary." Alec crossed his arms over his chest and surveyed the energy in the room. "Just took a little time."

"And a little motivation?" Bracing himself on the back of one of the metal folding chairs, Billy glanced at him and jerked up his chin.

Alec punched him playfully in the shoulder. "Maybe, but it had nothing to do with your threat to pass out my phone number."

"If you say so." Billy grinned, then his face sobered. "How's Sarah?"

"I believe she's being discharged today."

"Good to hear." His brother-in-law straightened and slid a hand into his front pocket. "You know, that opening is still available if you'd like to come back to the department."

"Thanks, but I'm happier selling houses than saving them. What you do is amazing and heroic, but I think God has something else in store for me." He told Billy about his plans for the building.

"Christy would be pleased."

"I'm sure. Hey, man. I loved your sister, and I'll always cherish our time together, but I can't continue living in the past. I'm starting over. If Sarah and the boys will let me, I hope to be a part of their lives."

"I know you're not asking for my blessing, but I'm giving it anyway. You'll always be family."

"Thanks, man. That means a lot. And since you're family and all, how about lending a hand to help me win back the girl?"

"Whatever you need."

He needed Sarah, and he prayed she'd be able to see he was the right man for her.

Sarah had never been a crybaby. Even after Adam broke her heart, married someone else and announced their pregnancy, she hadn't cried more than two days total.

But as she stood in front of the mirror and tried to apply makeup to cover the bruises and abrasions on her face, she couldn't stop the stream of tears flowing down her cheeks and smearing her mascara.

She looked like a freak with her smoke-reddened eyes, singed hair and parched skin.

How was she supposed to put on a happy face and smile through dinner? Sniffling, she reached for a tissue off the counter and wiped the smeared makeup.

She'd honestly expected the church board to continue the program. After arriving at Nate and Melissa's, she'd pressured Nate for details… Melissa had been right—finances were the main concern. At least he did promise to explore new options next week as long as she promised to relax and not think about it.

If it weren't for the boys, she'd consider trying to finance it herself, but with legal costs and needing to prove financial responsibility, it looked as if she'd have to say yes to Jonah's job offer after all. And start over. Again. Would the boys be willing to move to Virginia?

The thought made her stomach churn. But she had to push it out of her head for now.

Caleb and Zoe were arriving any minute to pick her up for a dinner she didn't even have an appetite for—and she wasn't close to being ready.

She dotted more concealer under her eyes and

blended it with her pinky. Well, it had to be good enough. Maybe the restaurant would have dark lighting to hide her flaws.

She shed her pajamas and slipped into a pink sundress, white shrug and white wedges. She hung an enamel daisy necklace around her neck and hooked white hoops in her ears. Maybe the fun jewelry would brighten her mood.

After napping at Melissa and Nate's, Caleb had picked her up and taken her home, giving her Daniel's key to unlock her apartment. With no car, no phone and no purse with her bank cards, she was pretty much stuck at the apartment. Not that she cared to go anywhere anyway. Tomorrow she'd apply for a new driver's license and bank cards. Maybe Caleb could help her figure out what to do about her car, which had been crushed in the back parking lot when the tree had come down.

But even though she was here, Alec hadn't bothered to come see her and make sure she was okay. She didn't even hear Eliza barking downstairs.

And it bothered her more than she cared to admit.

That awareness brought a quick rush of tears. And that made her angry. She wasn't going to cry over someone who couldn't even take two minutes to stop in and say hi, even if she hadn't seen him in over a week.

Jerk.

She sat on the edge of the tub and cradled her forehead in her hands. She really didn't feel like going out. She wasn't going to be good company, so maybe she should just cancel. With no phone, she'd have to wait until Caleb showed up, but then he'd convince her to get out and get some fresh air.

Why would he even suggest going out in public on the day she was released from the hospital?

Because he knew she needed the distraction. Otherwise, she'd continue reliving the nightmare all over again. Despite two showers, she continued to smell the lingering stench of smoke in her hair. The doctor said her cough should improve in a couple of days once her irritated lungs healed.

Now she understood what Alec meant when he'd said the fire haunted him. But she didn't want to spend the rest of her life afraid.

A knock sounded on her door. She trudged through the living room and opened it. Caleb stood on the landing, wearing his typical untucked white button-down shirt and khaki shorts. He smiled. "Ready?"

She kept a hand on the door. "Listen, Caleb, I'm not feeling so great. I think I should skip dinner."

"You need to eat. The kids have been so worried about you. I don't want to ruin any surprises, but the girls made you something. Let's just say our house is covered in glitter and Disney stickers."

Sarah blew out a sigh. Her brother's veiled guilt trip worked. "Fine, but I can't be held responsible for any grumpiness that may ensue."

"Noted."

She reached for her purse only to remember it had burned in the fire. One more thing to add to tomorrow's to-do list. She grabbed Daniel's key and locked the door, then realized she didn't have a pocket to hold it. Caleb could keep it in his pocket for her.

She expected to find their SUV loaded with Zoe and the kids. Instead, Caleb's sedan waited at the curb. "Where is everyone?"

"They're meeting us downtown. With Daniel and Toby, we didn't have enough room for all of us. I figured if you wanted to cut out early, I could run you home without loading up everyone else."

"Thanks, I appreciate it."

They drove the few blocks to the business district. Cars lined both sides of Center Street, which was unusual for a weekday evening in the small town. Caleb circled the block again, then slid into a spot in front of Cuppa Josie's. People lined the sidewalk. Music spilled from one of the nearby buildings.

What was going on?

"Where are we going for dinner? I didn't think to ask, and you didn't say."

"No, I didn't." He flashed her the same grin that always managed to get him out of trouble with his wife. He shifted the car into Park and shut off the engine.

She opened her door and followed him onto the sidewalk and then hurried to keep up with his long-legged stride as he pushed through the crowd gathered on the sidewalk.

He stopped in front of Alec's late wife's business, Christy's Closet. The storefront windows no longer showcased posed mannequins dressed in stylish clothes. White café curtains hung in the windows, and she was able to see tables and people even before they opened the door.

She shot Caleb a puzzled look. "What's going on?"

"Let's go in and find out." Caleb opened the door, then stepped back for her to pass through.

Applause, cheers and whistles greeted her. People swarmed around her, grabbing her hand, hugging her and asking a million questions about how she was doing. They herded her deeper into the room.

Where was Caleb? Or Zoe?

She'd never been afraid in crowds before, but all of a

sudden the walls appeared to be closing in on her. Her breathing hitched in her chest as her stomach quivered. She needed everyone to back up. She needed air.

Her eyes darted around the room, searching for an escape. Someone from behind gave her upper arms a gentle squeeze and whispered in her ear, "Sarah."

Recognizing Alec's voice, she turned, buried her face into his chest and mumbled into his shirt.

He lowered his head. "What was that?"

"Get me out of here. I need some air."

Alec wrapped an arm around her shoulders and drew her to his side while fighting his way through the maze of tables covered with white tablecloths and decorated with clear vases filled with wildflowers. He led her out the back door into a private parking lot. The heavy steel door closed behind them, shutting out the din of conversation and music.

He pulled out his keys and unlocked his car. Opening the passenger door, he guided her onto the leather seat.

She pressed her head against the back of the seat, suddenly feeling a little foolish. She drew in several deep breaths, and the screaming in her head quieted down.

Alec squatted beside her and brushed her hair off her cheek. "You okay?"

She nodded, but didn't open her eyes. "I've never had an anxiety attack in public, but all of a sudden I felt trapped."

"Like you were back at the center?"

"Yes."

"You need to see someone. You don't want that traumatic experience haunting you."

"Talking from experience?"

"Something like that."

Sarah turned her head and looked at him. She hadn't seen him in over a week. The same lines creased his forehead. His eyes reminded her of her favorite worn jeans. His hair had been cut recently. He looked the same, yet something was different. He seemed less… wired…more peaceful than she'd ever seen him.

Or maybe her head was messing with her again.

He traced her jaw with his index finger. "How are you feeling?"

"Honestly?"

"Of course."

"Tired. Very tired. Every time I try to sleep, I hear the crash, smell the smoke, feel the flames. I was so scared." Her voice caught in her throat as she forced back the pressure building behind her eyes.

"Come here." Alec slid his hands under her arms and practically lifted her out of the car. He pulled her into his embrace and tightened his arms almost as if he was afraid to let her go. He kissed the top of her head, then whispered into her hair, "Thank God, you're safe, Sarah."

She wanted to melt into his arms and allow his strength to support her, but her heart cried out at his nearness, knowing they couldn't be together. She'd be leaving soon. But for a moment, she breathed in his closeness, memorizing the way they fit together so perfectly.

If only.

Chapter Seventeen

"What's going on, Alec?" Gently Sarah stepped away from him, suddenly feeling cold and missing him even though he was only a foot away from her.

"With what?"

She waved a hand toward the building. "With this. The dinner."

Alec scrubbed a hand over his face. "There's a lot I need to say to you, but not here…not like this. I know you're exhausted, but promise me we can talk later."

"I don't know if that's a good idea."

"Please, Sarah, it's important."

"Answer one thing."

"Anything."

"Where were you? Did this summer mean so little to you that you couldn't even check to make sure I was okay?" She didn't mean to blurt it out like that, to expose the vulnerable side of her heart, but the question weighed so heavily that she needed to ask it or sink under the weight of it.

Alec stepped forward and crushed her to his chest. "Oh, my sweet Sarah, nothing could be further from the truth. I nearly lost it when I learned you were trapped in that building. My worst nightmare happening all over again, and I was helpless. I didn't come to see you because I had to take care of some unfinished business. That's what I need to talk to you about. Will you come to my place after the dinner so we can talk?"

The idea of talking when she knew it couldn't change anything had her hesitating. "I don't know, Alec."

"Please, Sarah. I really need you to hear me out." Desperation fringed the edges of his throaty voice.

She wrapped her arms around her waist and dropped her voice to nearly a whisper. "And I really needed you there for me."

"I know. And I'm sorry. If you listen to what I have to say, then maybe you can forgive me."

She sighed. "Okay, fine."

"Thank you." He brushed his lips across her temple, then rested his forehead to hers. "I missed you. So much."

She missed him, too, but she stayed quiet. Otherwise, walking away from him was going to be harder than ever. She'd hear him out tonight, but she'd have to pray for strength to stand against his wish for them to be together.

The back door flung open.

Alec dropped his hands and stepped away from her as Chloe stepped outside. "Hey, you two. The party's inside. Everyone's asking about Sarah, including a friend of yours… Jonah?"

Sarah's hand flew to her mouth. "With everything happening, I forgot he was coming." She looked at Chloe and smiled. "Thanks. Will you tell him I'll be right there?"

"Sure thing." She disappeared back inside.

Sarah turned to follow, but Alec grabbed her hand.

"Sarah, wait. Jonah's your friend who's the mission director, isn't he?"

"Yes, he called the other day to ask if I'd made a decision."

"Have you?"

"Not yet. I invited him to come to the dinner before everything fell apart."

He enveloped her hand between his. "Please don't commit to anything until after we talk."

"I won't."

"Good." Alec released her hand, then opened the door so they could slip back inside.

She greeted Jonah with a hug, but before she could introduce him to anyone, Amber, Garrett, Daniel, Toby and the other teens dressed in black pants, white shirts and white aprons rushed to greet her.

Amber threw her arms around her, nearly hitting Garrett in the eyebrow. "Miss Sarah, we're so glad you're safe. We've been like praying and stuff."

She gathered them into a group hug. "Thanks, you guys. Now can someone tell me what we're celebrating?"

Daniel frowned. "You don't know?"

"Not a clue."

"It's our community dinner."

"But how?"

Garrett jerked a thumb over his shoulder to where Alec leaned a shoulder against the wall, watching them. "Mr. S. is da man. He helped us pull it off."

"Alec did this?"

"We all pitched in, but it was definitely like his idea and stuff." Talking over each other, they told her about their talk with Alec, the way they'd divided into teams and how he'd made everything come together.

The more they talked, the more her heart stretched until she felt as if it would explode. From the time she'd met him, she'd prayed he'd be able to cast aside his prejudices to see what great kids they were. It appeared God had answered her prayers.

Sarah glanced over to where Alec had been standing, but he wasn't there. She scanned the crowd, spotting Stephen and Lindsey Chase talking with Nick and Josie Brennan and Ian and Agnes James. She waved to Gran and blew kisses to her nieces, Ella and Ava.

But still no Alec. She'd find him later and express her deepest appreciation.

Ella and Ava, dressed in matching multicolored polka-dot sundresses and white sandals, raced across the room, waving papers and calling her name. "Auntie Sarah, we made you cards."

She bent down and gathered them to her chest, inhaling the sweet scent of their shampoo. Tears pricked her eyes again when she thought about how she might have lost them forever. She needed to stop thinking that way. She was safe. She sniffed and smothered their cheeks with kisses. "Hey, my cutie patooties, how are you doing?"

"We made you cards," Ella repeated.

"That was so sweet of you. How about if we go and sit so I can read them?"

The girls scampered ahead and Sarah followed. After giving Zoe a quick hug, she sat between the girls and made noises of appreciation over the cards. Caleb hadn't been kidding about the glitter or stickers.

"Excuse me. May I have your attention?"

Sarah pulled her gaze away from the girls to find Daniel standing near the food tables, his cheeks as pink as her sundress. "On behalf of our summer outreach program, we want to say thanks for coming and supporting us. And thanks to the Shelby Lake Community Church for believing in us. But we'd especially like to thank Sarah Sullivan and Alec Seaver for teaching us that cooking is more than making food." Daniel paused and pulled an envelope out of his back pocket. "If Sarah and Alec will come here, we have a small gift of appreciation for them—a gift card for dinner at the Lakeside Lodge."

Sarah blinked back tears as she made her way to Daniel and gave him a quick hug. "Thanks, you guys, but this was totally unnecessary."

"You've given us so much this summer that we wanted to give something back."

Sarah wiped wetness from the corner of her eye with her index finger. She didn't need to talk with Alec before giving Jonah her decision.

Shelby Lake was her home. She couldn't leave. Even if the church board didn't agree to continue the program, God had a plan for her. She'd simply have to trust Him to work everything out. He'd be with her no matter what happened.

Alec couldn't have asked for a better evening.

The dinner had been a success. Their friends and family had raved about the teens' skills and, thanks to Billy's connections, the event had been picked up by the local media.

With the clock creeping toward midnight, he unlocked his front door. Eliza greeted him by bounding toward him and dancing around in circles until he picked her up.

He kicked off his shoes and stretched out on the couch with the dog on his chest licking his chin.

The doorbell rang, sending Eliza sailing off the couch and barking like a fluffy ball of terror. Alec's heart picked up speed as he moved to his feet.

Please, God, help Sarah see I'm the right one for her.

Blowing out a breath, Alec scooped up the pup and opened the door.

Sarah stood under the glow of the porch light. She had changed out of her dress into denim shorts and a white T-shirt. "Hey, you. Come in."

"Thanks." Stepping inside, she avoided his eyes. Instead, she lifted Eliza out of his arms and buried her face in the dog's fur. "I missed you so much."

What about him? Had she miss him? Even a little?

Eliza replied by licking Sarah's neck. She laughed—a sound that sent his heart skipping across his ribs.

Alec gestured toward the couch. "Have a seat. Would you like some iced tea?"

"Sure, that sounds great."

The temperature in the room seemed to have cooled a bit since Sarah had stepped into his house. Was he wasting his time trying to talk to her? She needed to hear what he had to say, but it seemed as though she'd built a wall between them. He had no one to blame but himself. Hopefully, though, he could also be responsible for tearing it back down.

He headed into the kitchen, filled two glasses with ice, reached for the pitcher of tea then stopped.

What was he doing?

He set the glasses on the counter, strode into the living room, scooped Eliza off Sarah's lap and set her on the couch. Taking Sarah's hand, he pulled her up gently and into his arms. He caressed her bruises and brushed a faint kiss over her cheeks. "You are so beautiful."

Her eyes searched his face, but she remained silent.

He slid her hair behind her ear. "I waited all evening to do this, and I can't wait a second longer." Alec cupped her face and stroked her incredible cheekbones with his thumbs. Her lips parted slightly as she looked up at him. He lowered his head and kissed her.

Slowly her arms curled around his neck. Her fingers toyed with the hair at his nape. He stifled a shiver.

Cradling her against his chest, he never wanted to let her go again. Her silky hair brushed against his chin. He drew in a lungful of air, breathing in her fragrance, which offered a soothing balm to his soul.

Drawing back, he looked into her eyes. "Sarah Sullivan, I love you."

She opened her mouth, but Alec pressed a finger to her lips. "Before you say anything, please hear me out."

He sat on the couch and pulled her down beside him. For the next half hour he shared about the fire's aftermath—reading Justin's letters, crying out to God and ending up at Nate's place. He told her about Chloe and Jane Lynn cleaning out Christy's Closet. "I couldn't have done any of this without you, Sarah, and for that I'm grateful. I love you."

Sarah's eyes glistened. Instead of replying with the three words he longed to hear, she reached over and stroked Eliza's fur. Then she dropped her gaze to her lap and picked at her reddened, broken fingernails damaged from trying to pry the storage room door open.

Was he too late? Or maybe she'd never felt the same way about him. If that was the case, then he'd just made a huge fool of himself. No, he refused to believe that. He had a pretty good read on people when his judgment wasn't clouded.

Sarah cared for him.

He couldn't take it anymore. He tipped her chin up to meet her eyes. "Say something, please."

She took his hand in hers and stroked his fingers, one by one. "I'm trying to process everything you shared." She looked at him with eyes that sparkled like morning dew on the grass. "I'm so happy for you, Alec. I truly am. When I saw you at the dinner tonight, something about you seemed different, and now I know why."

He appreciated her words, but he sensed they were about to be punctuated with a *but*.

"But…"

There it was.

He wanted to jump in and reassure her nothing stood in their way. Instead of speaking, he stayed quiet and waited for her to speak her mind.

"My life is going to be changing in a big way. I've decided to adopt Daniel and Toby, so I come as a package deal. We're all going into therapy. The boys are still grieving the loss of their parents and their grandma. I'm having nightmares about the fire. Truth is, we're a mess. I can't ask you to take that on just as you're coming out from under your own trials."

"A while ago, you suggested I talk with someone about my PTSD. I have an appointment next week. Dr. Wheeler is a Christian counselor." Alec slipped his wallet out of his back pocket, pulled out a business card and handed it to her. "If you're looking for suggestions, consider his practice."

"Thanks." She smiled and cupped his cheek. "I'm so glad for you. I know you'll do well. But are you really sure you're ready to commit to someone else? What about the boys?"

Alec laced his fingers through hers. "I promise there's no resentment of any kind. I realize now that

Justin was a broken kid, not the norm. I told you before, but I'll say it again—Christy was my first love, and she will always hold a special place in my heart. But there is a crazy amount of room for you. And finally, no matter what the church board decides, the outreach program will continue."

"How so?" She frowned.

Alec grinned, finally thrilled to release the secret he'd been holding for a few days. "I now own the building where Christy's Closet used to be—I bought it from Gran. After Christy's death, I banked her life insurance money. I've talked with Nick Brennan about setting up a foundation…kind of like what he did after his daughter Hannah's battle with leukemia. The program will be funded from that money. I want to be there for you, Sarah—mess and all. We can take things as slow as you'd like. Let me prove to you how much I love you."

"You don't have to prove anything to me, Alec. Your word is more than enough." Sarah pulled her fingers away from his, pressed a hand against his chest and rested the other one on his shoulder. His heart pounded beneath her palm. Her gaze tangled with his. He stopped breathing momentarily as a sweet smile spread slowly across her face. "I love you, and I look forward to seeing what plan God has for our lives together. Now kiss me again."

Alec obeyed immediately. Picking her up, he crushed her to his chest and spun her around. A startled laugh burst from her lips—a sound he hoped to hear every day for the rest of their lives.

Epilogue

With his heart beating louder than a bass drum, Alec rapped his knuckles on Sarah's apartment door. Without waiting for an answer, he opened it and stuck his head inside. "Sarah?"

"Coming," she called from down the hall.

He stepped inside and closed the door. The mouth-watering scent of freshly baked cookies lingered in the air. Stacks of boxes lined the living room wall under the window. Tomorrow she and the boys would be moving into Caleb and Zoe's house. Unless he could convince her otherwise.

She came into the living room wearing a long-sleeved purple dress with black boots. One side of her hair had been pulled back, exposing her graceful neck.

He let out a slow whistle, took her hand, brushed a kiss across her knuckles and then twirled her around. "You look gorgeous. Happy birthday."

Her laugh curled through his heart. "Thanks, you're not so bad yourself." She eyed his black pants and smoky-gray V-neck sweater and pressed a hand to his chest, lifting her lips for a kiss.

He was more than happy to oblige.

With her hand now tucked in his, she reached for her little black purse on the couch and slipped the narrow strap over her shoulder. "So where are we going for dinner?"

He held the door and touched the small of her back as they headed down the stairs. "It's a surprise, but I hear the chef is pretty amazing."

"Is that so?" She shot him a saucy grin over her shoulder and sashayed out the door onto the porch. "What if he sweeps me off ~~his~~ feet with his cooking and I end up running away with him?"

"I'm sure he'd consider himself the luckiest guy on the planet."

The autumn evening's chill bit at their cheeks as fallen leaves swirled across the porch and carpeted the grass. He guided her to the garage, paused to unlock his car and then helped her into the passenger side. He closed the door and then jogged around to climb in behind the wheel. Alec pulled a pale pink eye mask out of his jacket pocket and handed it to her. "Hey, how about slipping this on?"

She took it and toyed with the elastic band. "Why?"

"Because our destination is a surprise."

Smiling, she slid it on without another word. Adjusting it, she turned her head toward him. "How do I look?"

"Adorable." Alec started the car and backed out of the garage. His nerves ratcheted up a notch as he took several unnecessary turns lest Sarah guess where they were headed.

He parked in the driveway, then moved to her side to help her out of the car and guide her to the front door. "Hold on to my arm. I won't let anything happen to you."

"No worries. I trust you."

Music to his ears.

Opening the door, he led her inside. Sinatra's velvety voice greeted them from Alec's docked iPhone.

With her hand still tucked in the crook of his elbow, she lifted her nose. "Something smells delicious. Where are we?"

"Take off the mask and find out."

Sarah slid off the eye mask and gasped. Her eyes widened as her hands flew to her mouth. "Alec…"

She walked slowly across the polished hardwood floor, then stopped and turned in a circle, taking in the dozens of candles in pedestal votive holders flickering from the mantel, windowsills and built-in bookcase shelves. Bathed in the glow of the candlelight, Sarah's beauty stole his breath.

He shut the door, then moved behind her and placed his hands on her shoulders. The pleasure on her face made his heart soar.

Smiling, she shot him a puzzled look. "What are we doing here? I thought you said Emmett's house sold last month."

Alec stuffed his hands in his front trouser pockets and grinned. "It did. The owner was more than happy to let me use it for tonight."

He took her hand and led her into the dining room, where he'd used one of Aunt Elsie's embroidered tablecloths to cover the same dining room table that had been Uncle Emmett's first anniversary gift to her. He'd set the table with Gran and Granddad's wedding china at Gran's suggestion—she'd casually mentioned the milky-white bone china plates edged with tiny blue flowers could use a new home. A bouquet of wildflowers filled a mason jar—Chloe's suggestion. She'd rattled off something about Sarah appreciating vintage chic, whatever that meant.

"Alec, these are gorgeous." She fingered a daisy petal and smiled at him. "You didn't have to do all of this."

He took a step toward her, caressed a thumb across her cheek and dropped his voice to a whisper. "I wanted to."

"Thank you. You have no idea what this means to me." Squeezing his hand, she stood on tiptoe and kissed him gently.

"This is only the beginning." As much as he wanted to draw her into his arms, he left her side a moment, headed for the kitchen and then returned with a large basket wrapped in yellow cellophane. He pulled out one of the chairs for her to sit and then sat the basket in front of her. "Happy birthday, Sarah."

His breathing hitched in his chest. He forced his heart to slow to its steady beating. He shoved his hands into his pockets and curled them into fists. Was it getting warm in here?

"Thank you." She untied the yellow satin ribbon and pulled back the matching cellophane, revealing a hot-air popcorn popper. She burst out laughing, a sound that continued to make his heart sing. "No chance of me setting off smoke alarms at the new place."

"That was the idea." He nodded toward the basket. "There's more."

She pulled out *Roman Holiday* and *Breakfast at Tiffany's* DVDs—she was becoming quite the Audrey Hepburn fan—and then reached for a bag of multicolored gourmet popping corn tied with a yellow ribbon. "Oh, fun. I've never seen colored popcorn befo—" She sucked in a sharp breath, covered her mouth and looked at him with suspiciously bright eyes. "Oh, Alec…"

His eyes not leaving hers, Alec took the bag from her, untied the ribbon, and slid the key and the princess-cut engagement ring into his hand.

Kneeling before her and laying his heart at her feet, Alec reached for her left hand. "Sarah, a few minutes ago, you mentioned this house being sold. I was truthful when I said it had been, but what I didn't mention was I'm the one who bought it. You came into my life when I least expected…or wanted it. You're the sunshine to my cloudy days. You bring me joy and laughter. I love you with my whole heart. I know I promised to take things slow, but I can't wait to spend the rest of my life with you. Would you do me the honor of becoming my wife and allow this house to become our home?"

"Yes, Alec. Most definitely, yes." She gave him a watery smile. Her hand trembled as he slid the ring onto her finger.

Standing, he pulled her into his arms. "Dance with me."

Wrapping her arms around his neck, she looked up at him with those green eyes. "One small problem."

"What's that?"

"I can't dance."

He laughed and pulled her closer. "Then I look forward to teaching you."

"I love you, Alec."

He'd never get tired of hearing those words or repeating them back to her. "I love you, Sarah."

She rested her cheek against his chest. "How would you feel about a November wedding?"

He tipped up her chin. "You serious? That's less than a month away."

"Exactly." Her smile spoke of a future that promised very few dull moments. And he was totally fine with that.

"I think I'd like that very much." He wrapped an arm around her waist, cupped his hand over hers and led her into the kitchen. He turned up the music on his phone and gathered her into his arms, smiling when she stepped on his foot. "Dance with me."

He'd found his perfect dance partner once again.

* * * * *

If you loved this story,
pick up the first Lakeside book,

LAKESIDE REUNION

And these other stories from
Love Inspired author Lisa Jordan:

LAKESIDE FAMILY
LAKESIDE SWEETHEARTS
LAKESIDE REDEMPTION

Available now from Love Inspired!

Find more great reads at LoveInspired.com

Dear Reader,

How can we trust God when life breaks our hearts?

Alec and Sarah struggled with that question as they journeyed through their story. I, too, wrestled with that same question when life's challenges crashed down on our family. Like Alec, I struggled with forgiveness in a situation that still makes my heart ache. But I knew God was beside me every step of the way, and leaning into Him helped me to walk through those dark valleys. I simply needed to look up to see the light.

I clung to God's promises during those difficult times in my life. Sarah had her life mapped out only to have everything scattered. Alec went through the motions of living as he stumbled through a fog of grief. God had a plan and a purpose for their lives—to give them a hope and a future as long as they trusted in Him.

God sees you even when you're battling life's storms. He hasn't forgotten you. He has a plan for your life. When we align our hearts with His plans for us, He will use us in a way that captures our breath. Are you willing to trust in Him when life breaks your heart? I promise the reward will bless you beyond anything you could even imagine.

I love connecting with readers! Email me at lisa@lisajordanbooks.com or visit me at lisajordanbooks.com.

By His Grace,
Lisa

REQUEST YOUR FREE BOOKS!

2 FREE INSPIRATIONAL NOVELS
PLUS 2
FREE
MYSTERY GIFTS

Love Inspired®

YES! Please send me 2 FREE Love Inspired® novels and my 2 FREE mystery gifts (gifts are worth about $10). After receiving them, if I don't wish to receive any more books, I can return the shipping statement marked "cancel." If I don't cancel, I will receive 6 brand-new novels every month and be billed just $4.99 per book in the U.S. or $5.49 per book in Canada. That's a saving of at least 17% off the cover price. It's quite a bargain! Shipping and handling is just 50¢ per book in the U.S. and 75¢ per book in Canada.* I understand that accepting the 2 free books and gifts places me under no obligation to buy anything. I can always return a shipment and cancel at any time. Even if I never buy another book, the two free books and gifts are mine to keep forever.

105/305 IDN GH5P

Name	(PLEASE PRINT)	
Address		Apt. #
City	State/Prov.	Zip/Postal Code

Signature (if under 18, a parent or guardian must sign)

Mail to the **Reader Service**:
IN U.S.A.: P.O. Box 1867, Buffalo, NY 14240-1867
IN CANADA: P.O. Box 609, Fort Erie, Ontario L2A 5X3

**Are you a subscriber to Love Inspired® books
and want to receive the larger-print edition?
Call 1-800-873-8635 or visit www.ReaderService.com.**

* Terms and prices subject to change without notice. Prices do not include applicable taxes. Sales tax applicable in N.Y. Canadian residents will be charged applicable taxes. Offer not valid in Quebec. This offer is limited to one order per household. Not valid for current subscribers to Love Inspired books. All orders subject to credit approval. Credit or debit balances in a customer's account(s) may be offset by any other outstanding balance owed by or to the customer. Please allow 4 to 6 weeks for delivery. Offer available while quantities last.

Your Privacy—The Reader Service is committed to protecting your privacy. Our Privacy Policy is available online at www.ReaderService.com or upon request from the Reader Service.

We make a portion of our mailing list available to reputable third parties that offer products we believe may interest you. If you prefer that we not exchange your name with third parties, or if you wish to clarify or modify your communication preferences, please visit us at www.ReaderService.com/consumerschoice or write to us at Reader Service Preference Service, P.O. Box 9062, Buffalo, NY 14240-9062. Include your complete name and address.

LII5

"Are you sure you want Jacob to stay with you?" Esther asked.

"I'm sure staying at my farm is best for him now," Nathaniel said. "The boy needs something to do to get his mind off the situation, and the alpacas can help."

Nathaniel held his hand out to assist Esther onto the seat of the buggy.

She regarded him with surprise, and he had to fight not to smile. Her reaction reminded him of Esther the Pester from their childhood, who'd always asserted she could do anything the older boys did…and all by herself.

Despite that, she accepted his help. The scent of her shampoo lingered in his senses. He was tempted to hold on to her soft fingers, but he released them as soon as she was sitting. He was too aware of the *kinder* and other women gathered behind her.

She picked up the reins and leaned toward him. "If it becomes too difficult for you, bring him to our house."

"We'll be fine." At that moment, he meant it. When her bright blue eyes were close to his, he couldn't imagine being anything but fine.

Then she looked away, and the moment was over. She slapped the reins and drove the wagon toward the road. He watched it go. A sudden shiver ran along him. The breeze was damp and chilly, something he hadn't noticed while gazing into Esther's pretty eyes.

The sound of the rattling wagon vanished in the distance, and he turned to see Jacob standing by the fence, his fingers through the chicken wire again in the hope an alpaca would come to him. The *kind* had no idea of what could lie ahead for him.

Take him into Your hands, Lord. He's going to need Your comfort in the days to come. Make him strong to face what the future brings, but let him be weak enough to accept help from us.

Taking a deep breath, Nathaniel walked toward the boy. He'd agreed to take care of Jacob and offer him a haven at the farm. Now he had to prove he could.

Don't miss
HIS AMISH SWEETHEART by Jo Ann Brown,
available September 2016 wherever
Love Inspired® books and ebooks are sold.

www.LoveInspired.com

LIEXP0816